THE TREASURE OF Santa María

The Treasure of Santa Maria

Published by Tate Publishing & Enterprises, LLC
127 E. Trade Center Terrace | Mustang, Oklahoma 73064 USA
1.888.361.9473 | www.tatepublishing.com

Tate Publishing is committed to excellence in the publishing industry. The company reflects the philosophy established by the founders, based on Psalm 68:11,
"The Lord gave the word and great was the company of those who published it."

Cover and Interior design by Eddie Russell
Illustration by Genevieve Stotler

Published in the United States of America

ISBN: 978-1-60604-583-1
Juvenile Fiction: Action & Adventure: General
09.04.07

THE TREASURE OF
Santa María

by Seth Anawalt

TATE PUBLISHING & *Enterprises*

Contents

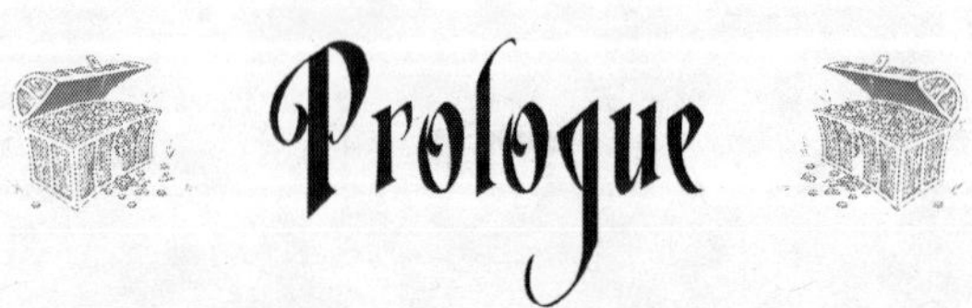

Prologue

[Western Spain in the late 1700's]

Four treasure hunters become rich, when one of them by the name of Manuel Diaz deciphers a map leading to the Treasure of Santa Maria, a vast sum of gold hid in the catacombs of an ancient monastic ruin. Fortune turns to greed, as Manuel is stabbed in the back by one of his fellows, a man named Carlos Carazo. Narrowly avoiding the same fate, the other men avenge Manuel's murder and later give his portion of gold to his wife, Francesca, leaving nothing to the Carazos.

Francesca's eldest son, Ricardo, inherits the fortune amidst a bitter rivalry between the Diaz and Carazo families. Coveting the gold, Carlos' elder brother Armando persuades his daughter to seduce Ricardo. Young and naïve, Ricardo succumbs and is forced into an unhappy marriage. His brother, Enrique Diaz, also marries and soon has a son who is Christened Fernando Diaz. Growing up in a climate of rivalry, Fernando gets into one fight after another with the Carazos. In trouble with the authorities, he escapes to sea on board a merchant ship headed out to the Caribbean.

A firebrand, Fernando is left behind on a small island where he encounters a group of monks living in missionary service. A Franciscan Order, the community proves to be just the cure for the youth's violent spirit. In time, he forgets his desire to roam and settles into monastic life. Meanwhile, another drama is unfolding in Spain where Ricardo dies (after losing his wife) and so bequeaths a vast estate to Enrique, including a chest of gold doubloons. Trouble follows when Armando Carazo (now a public official) challenges the will and seeks to confiscate the treasure.

Under pressure, Enrique ships the chest of gold to his son in the Caribbean. Getting wind of the treasure, Captain Clay and his bandits set sail from Spain and besiege the island. Departed to America on business, Fernando hears of the pirate attack and blames himself for the deaths of his fellow monks. Not wishing to return, and unable to go back to Spain, he travels the world and eventually buys a ship of his own, enlisting a faithful crew. He returns to Spain, only on word of Enrique's failing health. At his father's deathbed, he vows to return to the tropical island and rebuild the monastery.

Secret of the Lost Grotto

Margo couldn't share her find, even with the best of friends. It was a secret: her secret, treasured with every waking moment. She discovered the articles by accident during a family vacation to Lookout Mountain where she happened upon a hidden grotto graced with wildflowers and ferns at its entrance and seeming lost to time and overlooked by all but the curious young girl. Tired of berry picking, Margo wandered from her siblings on pretense of gathering flowers. She was led by a sense of intrigue: a desire for adventure common to the precocious eleven-year-old. The cave's mouth was narrow and only just passable by the slender girl who stood gazing with wonder into its silent air.

What impulse caused her to take the first step into the grotto's dark mystery she couldn't say. She might have turned aside and been contented with a handful of forget-me-nots. Yet she felt drawn by the hand of destiny into the rocky passage. Step by step, she made her way through the dim corridor toward a distant glimmer of light that cut across the cave at an angle in an inner sanctum lying beyond the long passage running straight as an arrow into the mountain's core. Often she looked back at the light of day that soon took the shape of a keyhole far behind; still she pressed on. Her desire, her mind, her entire focus centered on the inner light that banished the trail of darkness and lit her final footsteps into a large, airy chamber.

Before her stood an old silver chest that froze the awe-struck child, then drew her like a magnet to its finely engraved lid. Happily the light streaming in from an opening above allowed Margo's eyes to scan the unfamiliar lettering. Struck by the beauty of the writing, she was unable to comprehend the foreign script.

By now, they'll be wondering what's become of me, she thought, half wishing to leave and half wishing to lift the silver lid and uncover the mystery set before her. Turning aside as to favor the former course, her attention was captured by a small object that gave off a faint glimmer behind and to the left of the sealed chest. On closer inspection, she found the object to be a key hanging from a peg fixed soundly in the smooth rock wall. Taking the key in hand, she eyed it with growing amazement.

Had she not turned away from the ornate chest, she might have failed to discover the secret of the lost grotto. For the chest was well fastened and the key hidden from all but any who happened on the cave when the earth and sun were positioned so as to make the discovery possible. Embracing the key and its answer to her dilemma, Margo returned to the chest, feeling the sanctuary in which she stood to be filled with the watchful eyes of those who'd secured the dusty box therein long ago. Brushing aside her doubt, she lifted the key and with a slight tremor managed to slide it into the lock. The passing of years proved no impediment to the key's effect, for she felt the latch give way to the press of her hand even as she withdrew the key and slipped it into her pocket. How often since in her dreams had she experienced the same release and lifting of the lid beneath which was to be found the secret she'd come to cherish with the joy of youthful discovery.

"Margo! Margo, wake up, dear!" The sound of her mother's voice echoed in Margo's dream and brought her to the realization of the first day of school. For most children her age, summers in Witherspoon consisted of one long stream of uncoordinated events, punctuated by mealtimes and the varied demands of the adult world. A small community of five thousand, excepting the population surge during the town's annual hosting of the County Fair, Witherspoon might have been the beginning, end, center, and edge of the world as far as most people were concerned. Why the county had chosen a plot of ground an easy buggy ride from the town for its annual fair, no one knew for certain; it was just the way things were, and that was good enough for the townsfolk and those who came from far and near to experience the peculiar atmosphere of the fair. The kickoff to the week-long celebration of arts and crafts, games and competitions, livestock shows and the like was a foot-race beginning at Witherspoon bay and running a straight course through town and beyond to the finish-line flanking the main fairgrounds. On a good year, for the space of one glorious hour, the population of the otherwise uneventful town exceeded the twenty-thousand mark only to remain at its lowest level throughout the remainder of the fair, where many preferred to camp out than to stay at home, Margo's family included.

All summer long Margo preserved the secret of her find. The fair had proved an effective diversion, and for the space of that fun-filled week she'd almost succeeded in putting the matter out of mind. In truth, she desperately wanted to share the secret with anyone who might help her to understand its strange meaning. She loved her parents; yet there was something that kept her from revealing the discovery even to them. To divulge the find, she felt, would weaken its hold on her imagination. It remained a game, therefore, to keep the knowledge of the treasure from family, friends, and neighbors alike. People would come to know in time, she reasoned, and so wished only to keep the secret as long as her waning force of will allowed. Little time would pass before such willpower broke. Nor could Margo have guessed at the turn of events to come.

School began with its usual anti-climactic speech delivered by the rather round and flustered schoolmaster, Mr. Russet, who promised greatness to those studious children who gave themselves body and soul to learning and poverty of mind and life to those naughty children who wiled away the hours like the good-for-nothing grasshopper.

"And everyone knows what happened to the grasshopper and what became of the ant," he exclaimed. At which point, the flush of his face turned a deep red, followed by a general tremor of agitation that rippled throughout the assembly room like a shockwave, eliciting a collective sense of awe mixed with humor on the part of his hearers. Soon all eyes focused on the massive forehead of the towering figure from which poured the anticipated flood of perspiration that had the marvelous effect of calming the tempest of soul while cooling the temperature of body. Taken together, this proved all too much for the exhausted speaker who retired to his seat, mopping his brow with rigor of motion, like one wishing to fix a final exclamation point on the foreheads of his young captives. There, by some miracle of providence or the sheer force of energy expended by the impressive figure of Mr. Russet in much the same way at the start of each school year, it remained and bore fruit that even the local superintendent was forced to marvel at.

As for Margo, she sailed through the first week of school on the wings of a song: a melody borne on the ocean breeze and fading with each sunset, only to be sung again in a faraway land beyond the golden horizon. To this eastern skyline she often looked at the day's end, wishing for wings that might carry her to places only dreamt about. Little did she realize that the sandy shore on which her feet rested was the very land of her dreams. Earth, sky, sea, natural beauty, community: all this and more belonged to her by birthright. Perhaps in her heart she knew the truth. All the same, her mind often strained like a race horse, ready to carry her body into action at the least sign of opportunity. The signal would soon come in a manner unexpected, in the form of a stranger who much to Margo's relief would succeed in helping to unravel the mystery of her discovery.

She'd managed to keep the secret, along with the silver key, for weeks on end in the hope of solving the puzzle on her own. In Witherspoon, everyone knew everything about everyone else that could be known.

Hence to have a secret of this nature was unusual, if not extraordinary. Margo, with her keen wit and natural inclination to intrigue, sensed its value. She'd longed to share it with her best friend Eleanor. Clever and curious as Margo, this friend was all too aware of her strange behavior; yet neither she nor Margo would learn the real truth and hidden danger behind the mystery until the church picnic that Sunday, a day that blossomed bright and fair.

"All aboard!" Margo needed no prodding in response to the whoop of Deacon Jones, who knew from experience that a second call to the Whitaker's home would amount to a waste of breath. A clamor of feet, the foremost belonging to Margo, sounded from within the two-story house and erupted from the screen door, moving across the porch, down the wooden steps, through the flower-bordered yard, and up into the hay wagon where two dozen or so children sat upright on bales of hay, eager for adventure.

"Ready back there?" The words had scarce left the deacon's mouth when the wagon lurched forward on its way to Pirates' Cove, the odd choice of meeting for that year's fall picnic. Spring Creek, ten miles up the road from Pirates' Cove, was the usual picnic site. But fire, caused by the careless neglect of visitors yet to be traced by the sheriff, had resulted in extensive damage to the area of late, so plans had been altered. For many grown-ups, the idea of a picnic at Pirates' Cove came as somewhat of a shock. Yet with school only just beginning and the apparent sense of using the nearest available site to Spring Creek, objections soon faded and minds adjusted to the peculiar set of circumstances. No such mental adjustment was needed on the children's part. To them the news was too good to be true.

"Pirates' Cove!" they all shouted in a unison of excitement as the wagon jostled along toward its odd destination.

What does it mean? Margo thought to herself. *It all seems so strange; father's desire to visit a remote camping place on our summer vacation, my discovery of the cave and its contents, the fire at Spring Creek just days before our church picnic, and now the choice of Pirates' Cove.*

Her train of thought was interrupted by Eleanor, who cut through the mist with a wave of her hand. "Margo, Margo, what is it? You must tell me! I know something's going on. You've not been yourself lately. Tell me. Please, please! I promise, I won't tell a living soul."

Struck by the insistence of her interrogator, Margo glanced about in sharp agitation. She's managed to keep silent for weeks. At times it had been almost unbearable. She'd wanted to tell her friend, yet she'd felt it best to wait. Why? She couldn't say for certain; it was simple intuition. Looking over at Eleanor, she knew the time of revelation was near. *But not here,* she thought to herself.

"Not here, not now, Eleanor! Someone might hear us. How did you know?"

"Your eyes; your eyes give you away. And your behavior: not the normal carefree Margo I used to know. What's happened to you these past weeks? Have you seen a ghost?"

"Shhhh! I promise, I'll tell you everything. Just wait till we get to Pirates' Cove."

"But where at Pirates' Cove? And when?" The two spoke in whispers, not wishing to attract attention.

"Let me see. I'll tell you on the way to the sea caves."

"That old labyrinth haunted by the spirits of dead pirates? Are you crazy?" Eleanor replied, her enthusiasm waning.

"Eleanor, you know that's superstition. Will you go or not?"

Longing to know Margo's secret, and sensing the futility of objection, at length Eleanor acquiesced. "All right! But I hope you know what you're doing."

Picnic lunch, the annual quilt raffle drawing, a message from the Gospels about God's love for little children, a three-legged potato-sack race and other fun activities came and went. Margo and Eleanor decided to make their escape during the game of hide-and-seek when the grownups retreated for a time of rest in the shade. The children threw themselves into the game with heightened zeal, envisioning the specter of pirate fleets amassed like storm clouds on the horizon. So engrossed were they in play, and so engaged were the adults in conversation, no one noticed the absence of two friends who made their way through a long strip of forest stretching southward and joining in eerie union with the sea caves at the only entry point known by land. It was the girls knew a portal forbidden and warned against by all; still it was frequented on occasion by the stout of heart, though few ventured far into the dark recesses of the honey-combed labyrinth wherein the skeletal remains of pirates were said to revive and cut the throat of any mortal who dared enter their dark domain. Rumor also had it that stolen treasure lay in hiding along with the pirates' bones. Many had penetrated the twisted passages in hope of finding the treasure; some, so doing, had failed to return, leading local authorities to give a scientific explanation and everyone else to affirm the supernatural.

Margo herself would have declined the bold venture were it not for the map: the secret she'd discovered along with a second key somewhat smaller than the first. The old, well-preserved map included a set of four diagrams, one of which involved Pirates' Cove and what Margo knew to be the sea caves. It was, she supposed, a treasure map, including the original diagram of the labyrinth that had come to be associated with danger and death over the years. Like Margo, Eleanor had an inbred yearning for exploration. Both their grandpas had sailed the seven seas together and lived to tell tale after tale of harrowing encounters at sea and on foreign soil. Noting the interest of the girls, the retired sailors spared no effort in educating their granddaughters about the world of wonders beyond the horizon seen from Witherspoon bay. Over time, the tales had become part of the girls' souls. In the process, a strong bond of friendship formed that now carried the anxious companions in mischief along the final stretch of pathway leading to the cave's ominous entry. Once out of hearing range, the girls had entered into a conversation in which the full reality of Margo's discovery was related. The map, the keys, the description of the peculiar book left behind in the cavern, and chest: all was revealed to the wide-eyed astonishment of Eleanor.

"Now that you know my secret, you must promise not to tell a living soul! Promise?"

"I promise!" Eleanor vowed.

The oath of secrecy sealed, the two closed in on the gaping mouth of the caves with a mixture of exhilaration and wariness. Inclined to the west, the sun blazed a brilliant path of gold across the sea eastward to the horizon and beyond.

"Yes, it's the right time. You see, the map shows the angle of the sunlight hitting the inner cavern in the midst of the sea caves here." Margo held out the map and indicated the point of destination. She'd described the similar phenomenon that enabled her to navigate the mountain cave and to find the silver chest and its neglected contents. It had all sounded so easy to Eleanor: the direct path to the inner cavern, the chest in open view, and the silver key visible in the light on its nail.

"But this—this is different!" Eleanor announced of a sudden, realizing her and Margo's peril. "The sea caves involve a network of tortuous passages that could foil even the best of maps!"

"It's true; I thought of that too. Yet we must take the chance. To turn back would be to admit defeat before even trying. And you know what Grandpas Joe and John would say to that sort of cowardice."

"I suppose. But what about the lost treasure hunters? And the spirits of pirates who guard their booty?"

"Eleanor, you're not making this any easier. Come on; we must hurry if we're to make it back in time for supper." At this word, a strange voice sounded out, shattering the atmosphere.

"Supper you say? Aye, a good supper would suit me fine!" Margo and Eleanor froze in their tracks. "Don't be frightened, lasses. It's only me, Rupert the sailor, you see, come to your aid. Ah, but you seem to have lost your way, with map and torch and all, to boot. What might you be thinking, spying out them caves? Eh? Speak up! I ain't a deaf!"

The girls looked at each other in disbelief, then back at the apparition that emerged from the shadow of the cave's entry. "We . . . we were just taking a walk, sir," Margo blurted out.

"Y-yes, that's right, a walk," said Eleanor.

"Well then, perhaps you'll walk a stretch with me. I'll be thinking your kinfolk will worry up a storm should you two go through with your plan."

"Plan?" asked Margo, the map held close behind her back.

"Don't worry your pretty head, lass! First of all, you don't know the nature of what's took hold of you. My land, it's made a fool of you already!"

At this, Margo began to feel a bit ruffled, a similar look of irritation being evident on Eleanor's flushed face. "What do you mean?" she retorted, half wanting to turn and leave behind the odd figure barring her way.

"What I mean is that the thing has a hold of you, rather than your having the mastery of it. Don't you see? It's already led you in the way of great danger. How should I know? Well now, that might take some telling." Motioning to the path, the bright-eyed sailor beckoned the girls to follow as he took up his strange narrative. "You see, it was providence that brought old Rupert to your aid. And I shudder to think what might have come of you two had I not overhead them rascals."

Adjusting to the odd turn of events, the bewildered girls listened with growing interest as they retraced the steps they'd only just taken.

"Spied 'em out at their game of mischief, I did! Ha! To think, if only they knew, the culprits! I'll settle scores with one of their sort yet, mind! But that's another matter, and one to do with another pair of sailors. It all began nigh forty years back. I was no more than twenty and itching to be off to sea. But I wasn't alone in them days; no, indeed! There were two others I come to know—two novices, like myself, poor in book learning and ripe for adventure. And I've come to learn they're spry as ever a man might be. And shouldn't you know it, for the two I speak of are none other than your own grandpas."

A mutual look of disbelief on the dubious listeners' part met this announcement. "Never mind your doubts! It's a fact, is all. And you'll be thanking your lucky stars soon enough. Sure, I know your grandpas. Didn't we travel the world together? And didn't we part as friends not ten years afore the lot of us cast anchor for good? I assure you, we did. And it's been a long journey just to see the old mates. Yet what should I find?"

By this time, the girls had forgotten their fright and were focused on the elder's tale. "It were nigh unto two weeks ago, and I was sitting up in the midst of an old hollowed-out tree when I overheard a passing conversation: a plot that made me want to take the villains by the throats. By the throats, I say! And shouldn't they deserve it! Near I did spring from my place and dash their worthless heads together. But reason got the best of me, so I waited and took in the vile nature of their scheme. And it's good for you I did, else you'd a been headlong into them dark caverns by now—caught like careless butterflies in their net. To think! Curse the dogs! They're waiting in that deep, dank place still, waiting with blades in hand to cut your pretty throats! Mind my words."

Putting their hands to the tender place of description, the wide-eyed pair swallowed in unison and looked in wonder at their avowed deliverer.

"That's right, lasses! Well, I'd a stopped their mischief of fire setting too, had I the heads-up. They're a shrewd pair of devils, as ever lived and breathed."

"But why?" Margo inquired. "What does it mean?" The sudden display of courage impressed the wiry sailor, and he strained as to penetrate the question.

"I'll tell you. Not thirty years ago as we were cutting the breeze off the coast of West Africa, a pair of new recruits come aboard during a trade-stop in Malta got to talking big-eyed about a store of precious jewels hid some three days journey inland from the port where our vessel was soon to load and unload on course to South Africa before heading on to the mystical lands of the Indies.

"'That's it: diamonds big as your palm and other precious jewels to take a man's breath away,' so the one began.

"'And we've got the map, we have! Just lookee here for yourselves, mates!' the other boasted.

"It weren't but seven men in all set to staring at the map stretched out on the deck. The crew had a good laugh once word got round. But we were stricken: me, your grandpas, plus two others besides. The captain, a fair man and liked by his men, had taken the recruits on of necessity, having lost two men at sea. And glad we were, given the prospect of riches to be had at their lead. All looked bright enough. We'd have seven days at port, leaving time for travel to and from the treasure site. We were told that a collector of ancient scrolls and artifacts had sold the map unawares. Having researched the map's origin, the two men sought berth on the first available vessel bound for West Africa and so got both means and help for their venture."

Margo stared down at the map firm within her grasp.

"Aye lass, it' a copy of the same, that is, with some additions, I expect." The girls found themselves warming to the stranger and felt they might trust him. Had they a choice? A quick glance at one another conveyed the same question.

We must trust him, and I must know the story behind the map and its relation to my grandfather, Margo thought to herself. "You were saying, sir, about the treasure?" A smile met Margo's inquiry.

"I was saying, child, that we were stricken, the lot

of us, with the idea of becoming rich beyond our wildest dreams in the space of a week. Had the opportunity not been laid so sudden before us, we might have thought twice about venturing into unknown territory with a week's supply of food, a lone native guide, and two practical strangers at the lead. But we were a tough lot with nerves of steel and well used to many a danger on land and at sea. All might have gone without a hitch, were it not for the treachery planned by the two scoundrels. Sure, we were needed, but only as aid against the perils of such a journey." Drawing up the sleeve of his sailor's shirt, the storyteller pointed to a long scar running from the shoulder down to the elbow. "Here's the face of it! A tiger, sure as I live! It ain't no more, thanks to the swift action of your grandpa Joe. And it weren't but one of the many ill events and wild creatures that deviled our way from the start. It was as though the land itself had a mind to keep us from our aim, lest it lose its native treasure to our grasp.

"Damn the villains! Curse their vile plot! I'd as soon meet the same tiger that sought my life before losing its own as to walk in the shadow of such men again. But we did walk in their shadow, three days with only rest as to prevent collapse before we reached the point of destination marked out on the map. We'd traveled the most part along the great river, handing out beads to the native peoples for safe passage through their tribal territories. The second evening was spent pursuing a tributary that wound its way like a giant serpent through the deep green jungle where the tiger attack occurred. It's a wonder to me now that we covered so much territory in that brief time. No doubt the prospect of retirement from a hard life at sea was a factor in our determination. The sure-footed guide, who we'd happened on at the coast and whose tribe was the last to be seen along the way, also proved indispensable to our progress.

"On the third day at dawn we came to an opening in the jungle wall that brought us into the misty air of a towering waterfall that plummeted into a churning pool. It was clear from the map that the treasure was hid behind the massive wall of water at the spot indicated. Foot and hand holds had been carved into the rock face, allowing for the passage of one person at a time. This too was shown on the map. Yet it was here we made a fatal mistake: one that would cost the lives of two men and leave your grandpas and me near to the point of death. On we climbed, mounting a steep ascent stretching upwards along the north side of the falls. Reaching what looked to be a midway point above the pool, we stopped beside a great boulder that barred all access to the rush of cascading water."

"'This is it! This is the place!' one of the strangers shouted, raising his voice against the constant roar of water.

"'We'll need to cut around the boulder, as the map indicates, to reach the final path,' the other replied.

"We suspected nothing. We feared nothing. After two days and partial nights of travel, we thought only of the treasure and reaching our ship in safety. The hand and foot holds were there, to our relief. We thus faced the last precarious steps to our near fortune. If only we'd thought! If only we'd scrutinized the plan of approach and retreat proposed by the map owners. But we hadn't suspected, and so we went onward like sheep to the slaughter, your grandpas and me in the middle, flanked by two shipmates and then the two foreigners, one at the front and the other to the rear. We'd been led to believe the treasure was close enough to be passed hand-to-hand along a line of seven men spaced just so across the falls. All present were to keep their eyes fixed on the man ahead as we inched out across the sheer cliff. Only when the jewels had been found were we to look back and forth while passing them, pouch by pouch, along the wall. To this day, I can't say for sure who acted first; it happened as in a dream."

Had Margo and Eleanor been conscious of the church picnic, the plan of entering the sea caves, or even the ground under their feet, such awareness had since dissipated into the mist of the elder's story. As they moved along the cliff in their inner visions, the mist began to thicken, and for a time to shroud their grandfathers in a veil of death.

"Death came in a moment to the men on either side of your grandpas and me. The cries could not be heard on account of the thunderous roar of the falls. It was a shot, no doubt: two consecutive shots calculated to go off at the same time, one from the rear and the other the front of the line. Perhaps the timing was chance; I can't be sure. The men fell, one after the other, like worthless objects to be cast aside once their use had been spent. We three would have perished in the same manner had it not been for the iron-willed resolve and fearless attitude ingrained in our souls from years of hard service at sea. What a sight it must have been: the three of us jumping as we did before the devils could get off another round. They counted us dead for sure, at any rate. And stone dead we'd have been were it not for a lucky fall. Aye, had we come down just to the left of where we did, I'd not be here telling the tale, nor would your grandpas be alive today."

"But they haven't told us this story. Why, Mr. Rupert?" The directness of Margo's question and use of his name brought the wise old sailor to a stop.

"It's a hard thing to admit of failure, child. Even a robin has its pride. How much less a man? Then again, perhaps it wasn't time for you two to know."

"Please go on, sir." The request voiced by Margo's friend also impressed the burly seaman.

"Go on? It's a marvel we did! And sure as we'd have taken the two murderous thieves to trial, given the chance; that wasn't to be. Shrewd devils they were, they'd even anticipated the possibility of one of us surviving the plummet to re-climb the path and so overtake them. Climb we did, once our breath returned, but only to come nigh unto losing our lives a second time. For much to our dismay the scout had been paid in advance by the men to guard the ascent path. Good thing he was a poor shot. Finding no way round the rascal, we'd no choice but to descend and lay in wait for our rival's return. We waited in vain, nor did we learn more of them or the treasure for many a year.

"How we managed to find our way back to the ship in time for departure, I can't say. We felt the scorn of all aboard, along with a stiff reprimand from the captain. Had he possessed the nature of some captains I've known, we'd a been flogged senseless for sure. But he admitted to having let us go, though we'd not promised to return. And his mind was filled with other matters, not least being the sudden need of new recruits. He found them, and a seasoned lot, but not till we reached South Africa from whence we sailed on to the Indies and then back round the cape and north-westward to Europe and at length the Americas and home."

Home, Margo pondered. *I wonder where he lives? Whether he has a home at all? And does he have children? Can he even be trusted? Do we know he's telling the truth?* By her side, Eleanor entertained a similar line of thought, which she conveyed with a searching glance.

"I see you have your doubts, you two. That's good! Be on your guard; you never know when some cutthroats like them two waiting in that cave back yonder might sneak up and wring your necks like birds of prey." An uneasy glance backward accentuated by a joint tremor met this remark. "Well now, there's a sight: two bold treasure hunters afraid of their own shadows! No lasses, you needn't fret with old Rupert by your side. Though you'd be well advised to keep a sharp eye out for them two men; that you would. They're a cruel pair of buzzards, as ever fed on flesh. And many a man's breath they've stopped forever in their time."

"Please sir, we do believe you!"

"Honest, we do," said Margo, half wondering at her words.

"Never you mind! It ain't the reason for my warning. It's hard to stomach, sure it is, like as most evil is rough on a good-natured soul. There ain't no figuring it, in fact. It's just evil, is all. And them two critters won't rest till they get their hands on that treasure."

"Treasure!" the girls blurted out.

"Aye! Treasure the likes of which few ever laid eyes on. And it's here: right here under our very noses, if we but had eyes to see. Ah, if only you knew, if only you realized what it is you hold in your hand, lass." Glancing at Margo, the sailor pointed a weather-beaten finger at the scroll in its uncertain state of security within her grasp. "What I might have done with such wealth. But it's no use, for I'm old and have little time left. You, you have an entire life ahead. Perhaps you get my meaning? Perhaps you begin to see why I've come? You'll know the truth soon enough, I'd venture. Four days hence, when the clock strikes seven, look for it!" With that, their odd companion bid them farewell and vanished into the woods.

The Santa Maria

Cries of pleasure rang along the beach where the rush of happy children's feet coursed through the sand toward the beckoning waters of the cove. Did this company notice the absence of two members? If so, they didn't let on. Nor did they appear surprised when Margo and Eleanor emerged from the trees running headlong to the sea like two hide-and-seek players who'd lost their bearings at the game's start only to find them come its conclusion. They were at Pirates' Cove, and every odd occurrence served only to heighten the sense of intrigue and mystery. So the day wore on, filled with sandcastle fortifications and phantom pirate fleets pressing into the cove's deep waters only to flee with tattered sails in the face of fierce resistance. There were casualties, as one might expect, but more so by far on the pirates' side. At last, the people of Witherspoon were saved!

And so the sound of the adult bell calling the victors in for supper was greeted with a general sense of pride, especially on the part of two liberated scouts who'd been spared the sword's edge on account of an old family friend come to the rescue.

Be on your guard! You never know when some cut-throats like them two waiting in that cave might sneak up and wring your necks! The words, along with the memory of the day's events, turned over in Margo's mind. Eleanor, by her side in the wagon, was immersed in similar thoughts. It was no use; they'd just have to wait and see if the stranger's promise of showing the truth came to pass. But what would they say to their grandpas? The question struck the girls at the same moment.

"What will we tell them?" Eleanor whispered.

"Yes, what? They'll think we're just playing around if we tell them what happened."

"Perhaps we should wait," Eleanor suggested. "Maybe the sailor meant for us to wait. After all, he did say we'd know the truth of the matter. What else could it be but that he means to appear and reveal everything he knows about the treasure?"

"But why four days? And why the hour of seven? Are we to believe his words? He might be lying. It could all be a clever deception: the story of the pirates and all. Can we trust him?"

"Do we have any choice?" As it were, they didn't

have a choice, Margo knew. And there was nothing for it but to wait and hope for the best. Perhaps he had told them the truth. Besides, his appearance proved to be just one more in a related string of events that must, she felt, lead to a logical conclusion.

"I see your point. Okay, then, we'll wait. And we'll hide the map in a safe place where no one, not even the old sailor, could hope to find it. We'll know before long if he's honest."

"And the pirates? What if it's true?" The question had crossed Margo's mind. Nonetheless she shuddered at the thought: *Yes, what if?*

As Margo lay in bed that night, she reflected over the peculiar string of events leading up to the surprise meeting of the day. She'd observed her Grandpa Joe's uneasiness that afternoon. He was his usual talkative self. And none but a careful observer would have detected a change in his countenance. Still she'd noticed; for his weather-beaten face was a map, the surface of which she'd learned to read like a book—like the countless stories animated by as many and more facial expressions. Did he know? Had he seen the man who professed to be an old seafaring companion? Or did he merely sense the presence of danger? The latter seemed more likely, including the possibility of pirates. She longed to ask, in any case, and to tell of her and Eleanor's strange encounter. Outside her window the waxing moon lightened the night with its reflective glow. *I must know the truth,* she thought. *But how? What do the pieces mean?* Story after story, she recalled her grandfather's words, straining to find a helpful clue amid the colorful collection of tales. Sailing out on a sea of memory, she drifted off to sleep.

The days following the church picnic seemed to encompass an eternity of time. Pirates' Cove, the sea caves, the mysterious sailor, the treasure map and its alluring promise of riches, and the two villainous men whose shadows lurked behind every tree and corner waiting with swords in hand to lay hold of the coveted treasure all pressed in upon the anxious minds of Margo and Eleanor.

"Margo, Margo!" The familiar voice cut through the clamor of schoolmates whose carefree retreat marked the end of what to all but two was a school day like any other.

"Quiet! Do you want to raise suspicions?" This hadn't occurred to her spontaneous friend who glanced about to see if she'd missed a looming figure visible only to her questioner.

"Sorry! Its just today's the day!" The comment received an anxious look from its recipient. Yes, today was the day; and well they knew it as they made their way homeward; and well they'd thought about it with every passing hour of the week. "So, did your grandfather speak? Did he say anything to show knowledge of the visitor or even the bandits?"

"No, I'm afraid he didn't," Margo replied. "But he's not his usual carefree self; I can tell."

"I know what you mean; it's the same with Grandpa John. Yet he won't let on, not a word of it."

"We can't say for certain, but everything points to their awareness of the promised appearance, meeting, or whatever it's supposed to be. Come to think of it, Eleanor, my grandpa's not been himself since the beginning of summer."

"What do you make of it, then?"

The question which had surrounded the waking and sleeping hours of either friend was cut short by the sharp advance of a dark-clad figure who emerged, lion-like, from behind one of the giant cedar trees lining the peculiar roundabout route Margo and Eleanor liked to take home from school.

"Stop where you are if you value your lives!" A surge of fear mixed with an instinctual movement toward flight met this remark and would have carried the girls headlong forward had it not been for a stronger sense of caution. For while only one man could be seen, they knew the other couldn't be far away. Then too neither friend was willing to leave the other's side, lest one run into danger while the other escaped.

"Do ya think I don't know you—that I ain't got eyes to see? Aye, that I do! As I seen ya both with them grandpas of yours. I know you, young rascals! And don't I know them. Ha! The luck that spared their lives! No matter; it won't be long now." A coarse laugh punctuated this remark, having the desired effect of freezing the terrified girls in place and leaving them all the more defenseless in the face of the advancing man. In that moment, something of her grandpa's strength welled up inside of Margo, bringing with it the reality of his many narrow escapes. A plan, unknown to Eleanor, was taking shape in her mind.

"Please, sir, tell us what you want, and we'll be glad to help, really." A quick nudge brought a similar word of promise from Eleanor, though she wondered at her friend's sanity. It wasn't their first brush with danger, and it wouldn't be their last they felt.

Surprised by the child's boldness, the hardened pirate let out another laugh as he advanced and straddled the path. "So you will, will you? Come, let's have it!" The man's brute eyes bore down on the girls. "Give it over, or I'll cut your throats sure as my name's Jack! Give me the map!"

"Y-yes sir, we'll get it to you." Eleanor glanced sidewise at Margo in doubt, but was soon answered by a look that spoke of trust. "Only, we just need time. You see, it's hidden away."

"Hidden away, is it? Empty your bags! Be quick about it!" The girls obeyed, revealing a wealth of books, paper, pencils, and the like but no map. "Curses! Too clever to carry it about, are ya? I'll get it, just the same, or I'll have your hearts, do ya hear! And don't think

I won't find a way at you. See this scar?" The man pointed to an old scar that stretched from his left ear down across his cheek to below his grizzled chin. "Do you know who done it?"

"N-no sir," Margo replied in a guarded tone.

"Then, I'll tell you; it was that grandpa of yours, curse him! And what do you suppose I'll do to him and your other folk if you fail me?"

"You . . . you . . . you'd . . . "

"Aaat's right! So here's the way of it: you get the map, you get it, ya hear, and bring it round to the Mermaid Inn. You know the place?"

"Yes, sir!"

"Fine! Then see you're there by sundown tomorrow! I'll be waiting. And I'll be thinking on your grandpa and what he done me. Don't you suppose he'll be spared the same and worse if you up and peach. Now get!"

With that, the released captives fled down the path, leaving behind the receding shadow of the pirate, or one of the pirates, Rupert had warned them about. If there were any doubt, it was altogether banished and a pervasive sense of foreboding took its place. When sufficient distance allowed for ease of mind, the girls slowed to a stop and collapsed into a stretch of grass a stone's throw away from their houses, which happened to be on the same street in view of the bay.

"What are we to do?" Eleanor began.

"Do?" Margo stammered. "We're to find the truth,

that's what! And it's plain Rupert is a friend, and one who saved us from a worse fate than what we just escaped."

"Have we, Margo? Have we escaped? I feel as though a net were closing in all around me."

"Maybe so, but we mustn't be afraid. There's too much at stake. Besides, do you really think a man like we've just met would hesitate in carrying out his threat? Not for a moment! Not even if he had possession of the map! No, it won't do. We can't wait any longer. We must talk to our grandpas at once: they'll know what's to be done."

"Let's go, then," Eleanor agreed. "We haven't much time. And our parents will be wondering why we're late."

The matter was settled. They'd each persuade their grandpas to meet with them on Margo's porch an hour before supper. No one would suspect anything other than a desire on the girls' part to hear yet another story. And, as it turned out, both elders were glad as ever to oblige and so were waiting at the familiar place when Margo and Eleanor appeared, chores done, and hearts beating in anticipation of the help they hoped to receive.

"If it isn't a bold pair of adventurers ready to set sail and make for the open sea!" said Grandpa Joe.

"And a sober looking crew, as ever was," Grandpa John added, noting the inward strain masked behind the girls' uneasy smiles. The pressure, built up in Margo's case since the summer and raised to its limit by the scar-faced man at last came pouring out in a stream of words that got the better of the two elders and for a time left them speechless.

"Woe there! Easy you two, lest you get tangled up in your words and so defeat your purpose. What's this all about?" Joe's voice of reason had the desired effect of calming the tempest and bringing the crew to order.

"You first, Margo. You're the one who got us into all this to begin with."

Too unnerved by the recent brush with danger to take notice of Eleanor's evasion, Margo took the lead offered. "Oh Grandpa Joe, I didn't mean to get into trouble, honest."

To Margo's relief, it didn't take long to cover the details of the adventure that began in the lost cave and what with one event after another led to the fearful encounter on the road home after school. "It's the truth, Grandpa!" This declaration made the elders nod their heads before lapsing into meditation. It was a serious case, to be sure. And Margo felt relieved in an odd way in view of the concerned faces that reflected her final remarks. *They believe me,* she realized. *Everything will be all right.* What neither she nor Eleanor could have guessed was just how much of the mystery was already known to the pair of veteran sailors.

After a long silence and several looks back and forth

between the puzzled girls, Margo inquired, "What do you make of it, Grandpa?"

"Well now, I suppose you might say it all got started with the shipwreck off the coast of Spain that resulted in my meeting of your grandmother and bringing her with me to America. She died, as you know, giving birth to your mother, who I left in the care of my sister to be raised up in a proper home. Then came the journey back to Spain to bring word to Maria's family of her tragic death and news of the child. The fatal chain of events that led to our taking aboard the two devils spoke of by Rupert followed, spanning a seafaring period of about ten years."

"But why, Grandpa? Why did you never tell us this part?"

Joe didn't seem to mind the question; nor, Eleanor noticed, did her grandpa. "We would have told you, but the time wasn't right," he replied in Joe's stead. Long days at sea and perilous ventures had made the two men a close-knit team. It mattered not which was telling a story or what part one or the other might take up; it was all the same to them. And the memory of each, cured by the salty sea air and all too oft intense drama of adventure, was clear as the clearest south sea waters.

"Yet there remains a part of the story even Rupert doesn't know," Joe pointed out. "Though why he's here I can only wonder at. It came about just as he said. He went his way when we came ashore in America, nor did we hear or see aught of him for many long years. All the while, try as we may, we failed to put the thought of treasure from our minds. Not a week passed in which the memory of our betrayal in the jungle didn't bite like an adder. We were overcome, sure as the sun by night—stricken by a madness that can lead a man to ruin. At first, it was a slight affliction, an interest in lost maps, the keeping of journal notes including rumors of hidden pirate's wealth, or the whereabouts of sunken vessels thought to be filled with gold coins and other riches. The real sickness took some months to settle into our souls. And we, drunk with the growing obsession, in time gave way to its hold."

"It wasn't any use, like he says," Grandpa John agreed. "We were captives, sure, slaves to sin, as the good book says. No, there was no fighting it; the thing would have its way, or we'd be fit for nothing but the plank. Such was the nature of the illness that drove us and not us alone."

"No, by thunder! And would that it had been, ay John! Would that we'd learned our lesson the first time. But we hadn't learned, and ten hard years at sea had put us off-guard. When the break came, we were open targets for every gold-smelling shark this side the cape. It wasn't long before the secret was out, though just how it got loosed neither of us could say. But there it was, and there we were, sitting up with two shipmates making plans. The map was a chance find, not unlike the first map of the African treasure. Ours was a Spanish map, discovered during a further visit to my wife's family. Yet it was gold this map pointed to: more gold than a body, much less four sailors, would know what to do with.

"What happened then?" Eleanor asked, noting with Margo the awkward pause.

"What happened?" said John. "A mutiny attempt, that's what! Six crewmen, two of whom being our supposed partners in seeking the gold, took part. These two had organized the revolt so as to commandeer the ship for the treasure hunt. We'd not been privy to their plan. Perhaps they sensed our loyalty to the captain. Or they may have thought our plan impractical. Whatever the case, they chose mutiny and so risked the hangman's noose come the next port, which turned out to be on American soil. God only knows what might have been our lot had they succeeded: shark-bait most likely. It matters not; they were foiled and sent to trial where evidence of former piracy was brought out. Not long after we took leave of the ship to search out the gold, planning to make our way as soon as possible to the Caribbean island to which the treasure map pointed."

"Aren't you forgetting, John, the wound given the mutineer leader by my hand in defense of the captain; also the oath of vengeance he swore were he to escape the noose and find me out. It was the left side of the face, I recall."

"From the ear to the chin, like this?" Margo indicated, drawing an imaginary scar-line across her face.

"That's the place," Joe confirmed. "After all this time, to think!"

"But how, Joe? It's been twenty years!"

"A long stretch for a prison term. Still, it's possible, John. We never thought to re-visit the matter. No doubt our minds were preoccupied. Be it so, the authorities will deal with these men yet, I expect. In the meantime, you girls keep to the main roads. You hear?"

"Yes, Grandpa," Margo promised, not wishing to see the scar-faced man again.

"Heaven knows the trials we endured on the way to our coveted goal," Grandpa John admitted. "It was a gamble, sure, and we'd staked the better part of our earnings from years at sea on a vessel we'd come to call the Santa Maria. She was a fine ship, with naught but twenty years under her hull."

"We were anxious to sail," Joe recalled, "but could only do so after a month's passing allowed for a proper crew to be enlisted. The pains we took in choosing our help! It wasn't any use; we were plagued from the day we took to sea and found small peace till the day we set foot aboard a sister ship that proved our deliverance. I shudder to think: a cursed voyage, a crew that grew more irritable by the day, a venture doomed to failure from its onset. Why? Perhaps our motives were misguided.

"Whatever the cause, misery was our lot; it bore down in the form of afflictions that served to put every man on edge. First malaria, then an illness unknown to John and me set to ravaging the crew. Then the storm hit, sapping what little strength we had left and leaving us in its wake like a drifting cemetery in a sea of death. One, two, three, four men dead and given up to the sharks that swarmed about the wounded vessel in uncanny awareness of our state. By the passing of the plague and reviving of the wind, nine men in all had expired amid the foul stench of decay. 'Eaten from the inside out!' was the way most of the men described the plague's effect. This, however, was a mercy compared to the trial to come."

"A cry sounded from atop the mast," John rallied. "'Pirates! Pirates!' One, two, three pirate galleys, known by their black sails and brazen flags, came bearing down on our ill-prepared vessel and flanked us sore when they realized no resistance was forthcoming.

"'Stand by and drop your arms!' cried a stout, sour-faced man we took for a captain. This order was backed by a second leader coming from the starboard with another band of ruffians.

"'You're a sorry bunch a' sea dogs as ever was,' he declared. 'Which a' you swine 'ud be captain? Speak up or I'll have your tongues!' The crew kept silent to a man; and Joe and I, tattered and worn as the rest, gave inward thanks for the mercy shown. Then one of the men took up courage.

"'Captain's dead, sir!' he vowed, much to our amazement. 'Plague took him days back. There ain't no captain.'

"'No captain! No captain!' said the pirate. 'Ya hear that, Clyde? No captain!' A roar went up from the pirate ships. Were it not for the sickness and storm we'd endured, the pirate leaders might have spied us out and had our heads. But we were a ragged sight, the lot of us, and finding small plunder, they saw fit to take captive those young enough to be coerced into the ways of piracy. Of the seven remaining, two were beheaded by the man named Clyde, who appeared to take pleasure in his sport, two were cast alive to the sharks feeding on the headless victims, and three were left aboard without food or water to die a lingering death beneath the tropical sun.

"'At a way, captain, man your ship! Ya scurvy dog! The devil take the lot! Bah rum, and rot yer down!' The words," Joe grimaced, "growled by the pirate called Clyde as he and the others shoved off, added to the sense of shock and left us all the more downcast on account of our predicament. There was naught for it but to sit back and stare out across a barren sea. The sun faded. Night drew on, cloaking the horrors of the day. We three sat alone in the dark till sleep brought on by sheer exhaustion freed us for a time from our torment. We awoke to a gentle rain that washed over the deck and brought us to the reality of nature's demands.

We worked without a word, catching what rainwater we could and setting out fishing-lines in hope of satisfying our hunger."

"We were destitute and searching for any plan that might alter our plight," John added. "To man a ship of that size with three hands aboard would be nigh impossible: a fact the pirates reckoned. A weary week later, with no compass but sun and stars and no water left from the past rain, we began to feel the gnawing effect of dehydration. Soon the pangs grew worse, and by the ninth day we might have been stranded amidst a hot desert for the state of our souls. Faint from lack of drink, too tired to lift so much as a bait-line for the comfort of food, we laid back and waited for the end.

"Amid the fog of fatigue, near unto death, we heard a voice sound from what seemed a distance. Hurry mate, bring the bottle! Our eyes opened to the blurred forms of men who stared down at us in wonder while easing water down our parched throats. As the life-giving liquid penetrated our wasted bodies, the fog began to lift, and the anxious faces of those gathered about pulled us back from the grave. We were saved! Better yet, we were saved by a Spanish trader, the captain of which came from a village close to that of Joe's wife's family. Moreover, the name of the village was Santa Maria: same as our ship. When our strength returned, and we were able to meet with the captain, we saw fit to tell our story, from the first venture into the jungles of

Africa, through the long string of misfortunes that left us in the state in which we'd been discovered."

"As to the map," Joe concluded, "it was of no more value to us than a broken shell. We'd known hardship in more ways than a body ought endure. We'd been blinded, no doubt; but it wasn't just the gold, it was the selfish zeal to possess the power of wealth our coveted goal promised.

"It's no use, captain, I said, handing the bleached and wrinkled map to the man set before us. It's no good, our going on this way. Nor would I wish the curse of the treasure on any man.

"Perhaps we were right, he allowed, glancing over the map. Then again, it could be we'd been joined together by fate to finish a work that might otherwise have been left undone. He then asked about the third surviving member, whether he was under our command. Not any longer, I assured. Then, he observed, we too were free to carry out our venture, if we agreed to accept his aid."

The Island

"Margo! Eleanor! Dinner!" The insistent voice of Margo's mother rang out through the air, breaking the spell of the story and sending the girls headlong into the house at a dash. Gold fever caught hold of the eager listeners as evidenced by the speed with which they finished their food in advance of their elders.

"Well, I never!" Maria declared, staring down at the empty plates. She'd been given the name in honor of her own mother and had grown in time to look so much like her that Grandpa Joe, the father she'd rarely seen when growing up, often marveled at the resemblance. Yet she knew no more of her mother or the land from which she came than Papa Joe (as she lovingly called him) had told her. "Get along to your stories," she beckoned with a sign. "As if I could keep you from them, though I wonder they won't drive you both mad with adventure fever. That would be a fine thing, I dare say; lost at sea in search of foreign lands and fortunes, just like your grandfathers! Ah, but there's no sense in my keeping you from their history; it's yours as well, strange as it may seem. Go on! Go on!"

Margo loved her mother dearly and never ceased to marvel at her heritage. She belonged to Witherspoon, having lived her entire life by the bay, yet she exuded a passion of spirit that made Margo think of the grandmother she'd heard her grandpa speak of with fondness, the heart of Spain beating in her breast. *Maria! Santa Maria!* Margo mused to herself as she kissed her mother and turned to the door.

Once the girls were seated, Grandpa Joe took up the story from where he'd left off. "What good our venturing onward after the gold was like to bring we knew not, only that no worse calamity could befall us than what we'd weathered. We agreed to the captain's proposal, but only if he'd lend us men from his crew so as not to forsake the Santa Maria. Had she been given another name, or had I married a different woman, he might have declined. As it was, he straightway assigned men to the task. So we set sail on course for the island indicated on the map. The captain, a man named Fernando, oversaw a crew loyal as few we'd encountered. He even gave me a beautiful ornamented Bible enclosed in a finely engraved silver chest: a gift in honor of Maria."

At this, Margo sat upright and stared at her grandpa with a look of astonishment. "Did you say silver chest with a large book inside?"

"Silver as could be! It was a welcome gesture, though the Spanish script was difficult to read." Margo looked from one elder to the other and weighed the wisdom of revealing what she'd managed to leave out of her earlier account. It was no use; they'd just as well know the whole of it.

"Grandpa Joe, there's something I forgot to mention about that cave." Her admission was cut short by a wave of Joe's hand.

"Never mind, child. The truth will come out in due course." With that, Grandpa John picked up the story.

"One evening as Joe and I sat with Fernando in his cabin, harbored as we were in the bay of what looked to be a deserted island, the captain announced, 'It seems I owe you an explanation, gentlemen.' He went on to relate the story of our map, one that involved his own family. He'd joined up with the wrong crowd when a young man; drinking, brawling, and causing trouble. His father tried to set him straight, but his heart was hard as the world of bad characters he'd fell in with. At eighteen, he went to sea on board a Spanish ship called La Palma, whose captain was a friend of his father. After a year at sea and all too many fights, the captain informed him of his discharge. He'd be put off when the ship made port in Spain. Fernando swore inwardly that the captain would see the back of him yet, and that soon as they dropped anchor at the next island. As it happened, the port and harbor to which he referred was none other than that in which we sat listening as we did to his tale."

"The island!" said Eleanor, voicing Margo's like excitement. "Could it be the same: the island with the hidden treasure?"

"We were curious as you, Eleanor," her grandpa admitted. "And so I asked him: How do you mean? There's not a sign of life in this place, and it can't be twenty years since the time you mention?

"Seventeen years to the month, he replied."

"It wouldn't have been his choice to jump ship where he did," Joe noted. "On pretense of picking coconuts, he took leave and soon disappeared into the thick foliage. He'd not be found out, nor did the captain order a search. The ship weighed anchor and he remained. His plan was to take up with the next vessel come to port. Thus he watched and waited, living on fruit and diving for fish on the remote side of the island with a spear he'd fashioned from a suitable stick. He'd taken a knife, plate, cup, water-jar, poncho, and some dried meat from the ship, and it proved ample to see him through the first week. In time, he guessed at the monastic nature of the place."

As her grandpa spoke, Margo reflected on her map

of the sea caves and its additional sections including an outline of what looked to be an island.

"Fernando awoke one morning with a slight chill," John relayed. "He would not stand watch in his usual hiding place that day, as the fever prevented his effort of travel and by nightfall left him turning in agony of the ague. All record of this period was lost to memory, he avowed, so violent was the fever. When he awoke, after what might have been the second day, his eyes took in the blurry form of a small room with a table and pitcher. The vague outline of a wooden cross stood out on one wall. Candles burned at an altar. Then all faded till a rooster's crow broke the stupor even as the fever lifted."

"What became of him, Grandpa?" Eleanor asked.

"He stayed on at the monastery, so he told us, but he was only minded to do so until a suitable berth could be gained. Life was austere but good on the island. For the first time ever there was peace in his soul, he confessed. Two years passed as in a dream. Then a sense of unease became evident among the brethren. Trouble was in the wind, yet what sort they couldn't say. Only when news arrived from Spain along with a heavy chest for Fernando did the truth begin to unfold."

"The gold!" Margo guessed aloud, connecting the clues given.

"So it was," her grandpa confirmed. "And with it came a subtle form of temptation as into a paradise garden, and Fernando was none the master of it. A battle for his soul was in motion. And the monks gathered round who looked down in silence at the shimmering gold pieces knew the reason for the months of unease."

"Then his family was rich!" Margo offered.

"In a way, Margo," John replied. "For during Fernando's absence, his father came to great fortune at the hand of a benefactor."

"Yet the will of the benefactor was disputed by a local official, an avowed rival to Fernando's family," Joe furthered. "So you see, the father was forced to ship the gold portion of the inherited estate to his son in the Caribbean."

"Then Fernando's father must have learned of his whereabouts from his friend, the captain of La Palma," Margo added to her previous assumption.

"And sent the gold by means of this ship," said Eleanor.

"He did," Joe affirmed. "At first, Fernando was filled with a spirit of flight in hope of the reunion promised in his father's letter: flight from his island home and reunion on the foreign shore of America to which his mother's cousin had sailed after her marriage to a sailor from those parts."

"Sailor!" Margo exclaimed, looking with amazement at her grandpa. "Is it, could it be the same?"

"The very same, Margo. And we were surprised

as you to learn the truth of it. Though why Fernando waited to reveal the matter remained somewhat of a mystery. Maria had died, the family knew, as I myself had told them years back. They were also aware of Maria's child and its whereabouts in the Americas. In Fernando's father's mind the child had become a symbol of his own sense of isolation in the face of his oppressors and sorely missed son. Had Fernando returned, there would have been trouble the father knew. So at length, the press of circumstances led to the shipment of certain documents along with the chest filled with gold coins revealed to the searching eyes of the monks, including the brother who'd found Fernando and nursed him back to health: a giant of a man and former pirate known simply as Rodolfo. What would Fernando do now? He must, he felt, at least establish contact with his relatives in America; there the girl named Maria could be found, and there his family would arrive within the year."

"Witherspoon!" Eleanor announced, picking up on Margo's excitement and wanting to impress her friend.

"Just so, darling, Witherspoon," her grandpa affirmed. "And no farther from where we sit than the home in which Margo's mother was brought up as a child. It would be a short trip, Fernando told his fellow monks. The treasure was to remain at the monastery for safekeeping. Only later in America on route to our town was he to receive news of the trial and tragic loss endured by his monastic family. The pirate attack came a mere month after his departure. The leader, recognized by Rodolfo as the captain who'd put him off ship in time past, had learned in Spain of the fortune and its transport to the island, thus he'd set sail on course to the Caribbean."

As the girls listened, the specter of Jack appeared, and they shuddered at the memory of his words: "Give it over, or I'll cut your throats sure as my name's Jack! Give me the map!"

"Fernando's family never did make the crossing to America," John continued. "Instead, his father was accused of seeking to claim the estate and treasure without the proper documents of entitlement. Held hostage, he was unable to send warning or prevent the travesty of justice. As it were, the pirate ship and its captain, a man Rodolfo called Clay, reached the island in advance of the Spanish ship sent to retrieve the gold."

"On seeing the old cut-throat at a distance," Joe added, "Rodolfo urged his brothers to the secret hiding place beneath the main sanctuary. A portion of the gold was set aside as a decoy. But Clay was as shrewd a devil as ever walked the earth, and a command to search the monastery was given in spite of the ruse. All but five of the brethren sat in the hide-out. After a day's search, Clay resorted to a more direct method. But the monks refused to yield, preferring the torment of blade and fire to that of betrayal."

"As Fernando further related, Clay kept Rodolfo to the last," John went on, "forcing the former pirate to suffer the cries of his friends. When all failed, Clay had his men bind the giant monk to a large wooden cross that stood atop the steps leading down to the port. There he'd remain, whipped and mocked by the crew he once dominated, to writhe in the sun till madness from heat and lack of water might drive him to give way. Had the Spanish ship arrived a day later, Rodolfo may not have lived to tell the story. He was almost spent when the outline of the distant sail revived his hope. It was early morning and pirates who'd been hard at drink the night before were just stirring when the cannon sounded, leaving little time to do aught but depart in haste."

"But Grandpa, what became of the treasure?" Margo asked.

"Treasure? Oh, the portion was taken—carried off by Clay and his men. But the Spanish war ship, coming on the heels of Clay's exploit, was quick to pursue the pirate brig. A prolonged chase ensued, ending in the battle for which Pirates' Cove received its name. The brig was sunk and the crew taken captive after a fearsome fight. The treasure portion was buried beneath the waves along with the other pirate booty and so left behind by the Spanish captain. Yet he revealed nothing to the Americans, only that the pirates had been pursued from a distance into American waters. A map, later made by the same captain, indicated the location of the sunken vessel and also included an outline of the island from which the chest and its fortune in gold was spirited away. It was rumored that the treasure might be hidden somewhere within the monastery; and so other maps were drawn up, one of which I came upon during a visit to Spain, as you know."

"Surely Fernando guessed at the treasure's whereabouts," Eleanor insisted.

"Perhaps so," her grandpa granted. "In any case, Spanish crews and other gold-seekers soon overran the island, forcing the monks to relocate."

"We listened as Fernando finished his story," Joe concluded. As for me, he said, I felt like a man without a country. The indirect cause of his monastic brothers' suffering, unwelcome in his homeland, and bereft of all aid he left America in pursuit of a life at sea and came in time to purchase his own vessel. He did return to Spain but only on receiving word of his father's failing health. Only after their reunion and his father's death did Fernando sense a strong desire to rediscover the island."

"Ah, but the rest you know," Grandpa John concluded, leaning back in his chair. "As we've told you about the disastrous voyage that ended with our rescue by Fernando and his crew, headed as we were to the island on our map."

"The map!" Margo said. "The one we have includes

the island, Pirates' Cove, the sea caves, and a section covering the treasure in West Africa."

"That's right!" Eleanor affirmed. "Where, then, is the gold?"

Joe and John looked at each other and then back at the eager eyes of the girls, wondering if their granddaughters had learned the lesson they'd come to only by way of bitter hardship. "Treasure? Why, don't you know?" Joe asked. "The treasure is here in the heart."

The girls looked with doubt at their grandpas. "I don't understand, Grandpa. What do you mean?" At that instant, the hallway clock's familiar chime interrupted Margo's inquiry. *Dong, dong, dong, dong, dong, dong, dong,* it rang out. Seven o-clock! The girls looked about with eager anticipation, half expecting the peculiar figure of old Rupert to appear as by magic. He did show up, in a fashion, but not as they'd have guessed. It was rather a note, carried by a neighbor boy.

"Thank you, child," Joe said, taking the note and sending him off with a nickel for his trouble before reading aloud its contents.

> *If it isn't Joe and John reading this scribble! I'm the last mate you'd be thinking to hear from after all these years. Never mind that! There's no time! And there's bad news apart from the good I come to bring. By now, I speck the girls have filled you in on their part of the doings. Sure I was there*

to set their feet aright. It was my duty, is all. Yet we'd best take care as ever we value our lives. I'd not put it past them jackals to murder their own kin for a piece of eight. And it's no silver dollar I'm to learn about, no sir! Meet me at the Whale Tooth Inn this time tomorrow evening. Be on your guard! I speck the villains could be watching this minute. Keep a lookout! Be at the old place of meeting when the clock strikes seven. Mind the watchword. Bonita Santa Maria!

Rupert

"Well, I'll be!" said John. "What could that old salt-fish have up his sleeve?"

"No telling," Joe conceded, handing him the note. "Guess we'll just have to wait till tomorrow to find out. Rupert always was one for surprises."

"But why the secret meeting?" Margo wondered aloud. "Could he be in some sort of trouble?"

"He was free of harm when we saw him," said Eleanor.

"All the same, he's not one to play games. No, there's more to this than meets the eye," Grandpa John stressed.

"I'm afraid you're right. But we must think, John. We must put the pieces of this puzzle together, including the odd fact of Rupert's sudden appearance."

At this word, the front door swung open, revealing the graceful figure of Maria. "What was it you promised me, young lady?"

"Awe mom, do I have to?" Margo's question needed no reply. A kind smile and firm look conveyed all her mother's will. "Can I walk Eleanor home?" she pleaded.

"Very well. But come right back, do you hear?" The girls had flown down the steps and into the yard when the emphatic "do you hear" penetrated their space. They might have been leagues away on the island of their grandfathers' venture as nearing the pathway leading to Eleanor's house. "Oh, those two!" Maria sighed, shaking her head as she turned to the door. The elder storytellers, she perceived, were lost in a mutual reverie. *What a family!* she mused.

Meanwhile Margo and Eleanor were busy making plans of their own. It wouldn't do, they agreed, to be kept from the meeting planned by Rupert. And yet they puzzled over the designated place and words of warning. Had the pirates found Rupert out? Was he in danger? Why else his absence? Were their grandpas at risk?

"Oh Margo, what are we to do? We can't tell our parents. And we know Grandpas John and Joe would never take us along." Margo listened with a peculiar expression and distant look that Eleanor knew meant trouble. "Wait a minute! You're not dreaming up some kooky plan again, are you?" Still she remained pensive, leaving her questioner in suspense.

"I've got it!" she announced at last, turning to her friend with unnerving excitement that brought a look of caution to the latter's countenance. "We'll spy out the Whale Tooth Inn tonight when the moon's out and the old hoot-owl starts up. That full moon makes him nervous, I guess. It's good for us, all the same; he being our signal to climb out the window and meet at our usual place."

"What about the pirates? What about our promise to keep out of trouble?" It was no use; Margo had made up her mind and hoped only that Eleanor would be quick to see the sense of the plan. "Oh, why do you have to be so stubborn?" There was silence then an awkward pause. "All right, all right!" Eleanor submitted with slight irritation, realizing the uselessness of resistance. "But I don't like it, not a bit!"

"Then we're agreed," said Margo.

"We're agreed," said Eleanor, turning to run home at the sound of her mother's voice.

"Bonita Santa Maria!" Margo said in parting. "That could be our new watchword. What do you think?"

"Bonita Santa Maria!" Eleanor affirmed, dashing off, as did Margo, to homework, bath-time, prayers, and bed prior to the anticipated call of the owl and midnight rendezvous.

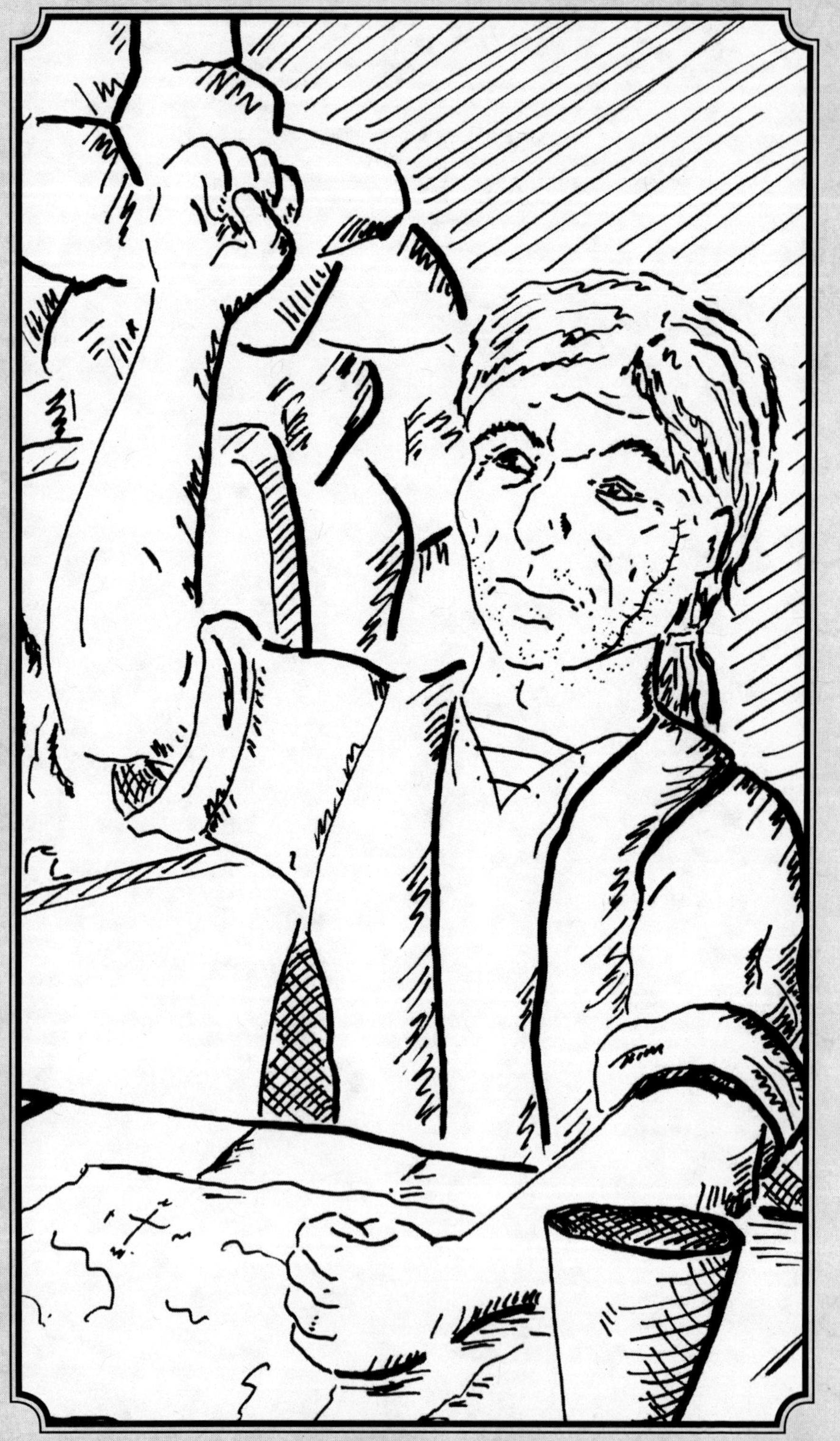

The Whale Tooth Inn

"What's that, Jack?" The inquiry came from a surly figure ten years Jack's senior. From his looks and the commanding way he carried himself, despite bad luck, one might guess him to be a captain less his ship and crew but not his pride. Yet pride in this case had been forged on the foul side of naval endeavors. One need only read the meanness of spirit etched in his grim face and note the same in his every move and dark glance to sense what manner of man he was and had become with long practice: ill-will that had meant the end of many a man's fortune and life, so many as to make murder and plunder mere sport to the questioner of Jack. The later sat in stony silence, glaring down at the map he'd sought in vain to decipher.

"Moved, I tell ya! It must a been moved! And them kids have our map, curse 'em! They'd best be here come time: time, I say!" The phrase was reinforced by a loud hammering of the scared fist on the table where the irritable pirate sat. The girls' map, he knew, was used to indicate the final location of the treasure. Rumor and fact placed the first location on the island from which Jack's fellow inmate, known as Clay by those in prison, had fled before being taken at Pirates' Cove by the Spaniards. The second site, thought to be a ruse of sorts by Jack, was that of Clay's sunken ship. The map, secured by Jack while in prison and followed to its fruitless end by the two men now laid up in wait at the Mermaid Inn, led to a third location in the far recesses of the sea caves. Yet this too had proved frustrating, leading them to suspect a further movement of the coveted gold.

"And you're sure about them two?" At this, Jack turned and frowned at his partner who, had they been elsewhere years back, would have just a soon shown him the plank as pay him notice. Clay remained guarded, however, knowing himself to be no match for his foul-tempered companion. From the day of their random placement together in prison a year prior to their release, Clay had played the role of confidant to this impetuous partner. Neither trusted the other; but such was common to their cast of characters. Shackled together by fate, they'd each remain aloof, knowing all too well their equal capacity for treachery.

"Damn me, if I'm not!" Jack barked. "And mark me, gold or none, I'll have the heart of the cur that crossed me! And wha' do ya think I'll do to that dog?"

"All in good time, Jack. All in good time."

"Time? You know, well as I, about time. Twenty years in that cursed prison! And weren't a day I didn't swear vengeance on him that done me."

"Easy, Jack. Once we've got the gold you take your vengeance. After the gold; ya see what I'm saying?" What Jack didn't see or know of was Clay's secret alliance with another ex-convict, a former pirate Clay planned to meet that very night.

"The devil!" Jack scowled, biting at his lip and gazing out the window at the distant flash of a lighthouse, enveloped as it was in pitch darkness. Clay, finding no response to this remark and wishing Jack absent, returned to his own searching of the night sky.

"Did ya know, Jack, I once heard tell of a treasure hid in the jungles of West Africa." The statement, uttered in an involuntary manner by one anticipating trouble, brought the dark eyes of its recipient round to settle on the object of their mistrust.

"What do you mean, Africa? And why bring it up?"

"The way I figure it, Jack, this here map we're after may be one more diversion, see. Now, don't get on edge. It pays to have a backup plan."

"Plan, ya say?" Jack muttered, staring out into the

night. A hot-tempered man, he was nonetheless able to pursue any lead that might prove profitable. "Go on, what's it all about?"

"About?" Clay lured. "It's about jewels, my friend: gemstones, diamonds, and pearls the likes of which you never did see. Jewels, I say, hid to this day in the jungles of Africa. How would I know? Well now, that's a question." Jack took in the figure of the old pirate as a leopard might its prey. Clay, who could read a man like a map, went on with his account. "It were a year or so ago when I overheard two fellas fenced up in the quarry, see.

"'Jewels, I tell ya,' the one began. 'And don't I know it! And didn't I come nigh to losing my life on account of them stones.' Sure as he'd trade his pick and them quarry rocks for them gemstones; that he would once he was out and free. So, he vowed, going on to tell of a traitorous partner: a man he swore found a map used in seeking out the loot. They found it, he bragged, afore leaving the treasure site on the heels of a native guide. The native fled, I heard tell, on sight of the jewels. The men trailed him, but soon felt the tips of spears at their backs. Led to the guide's tribe, they found the jewels of little use in bartering for their lives. It weren't gems but tools, knives, and such the chief demanded. One was freed, the other held captive against his return. Return? Ha, never! So the one was tortured, see, and made to carry the jewels back to the falls. How he escaped I can't say. The workday ended."

"What the devil! Ya mean to say you never saw the man again?"

"See him? Bah! Never, nor the other," Clay lied. "But I heard; and no mistaking his bent."

"Curse his bent! Did he say more? Did he give the whereabouts of the jewels? If not, why lead me on?"

Clay leaned back and stroked his wiry chin. "Aye, there was more; at the time I gave it no heed. Only later, as I sat in my cell turning things over in my mind, see, it hit me. A waterfall! The great wall of thunder told in legend where a vast treasure was hid! I'd heard the tale, sure; but forgot it for lack of a key to the riddle. And while I wouldn't swear it, I'd near bet my share of gold on finding them jewels."

Wanting to take the old liar by the throat, Jack soon thought better and fixed a cold eye on the man to whom he'd been shackled. "We'll see about that," he murmured, shifting his gaze back in the direction of the solitary lighthouse.

Meanwhile, in another part of Witherspoon, a hoot owl's call filled the air, penetrating the dream-space of Margo and Eleanor. Stirred into action by the signal, the girls were each dressed and out either window with barely a sound, leaving behind the familiar climbing trees and moving in anxious alertness toward the appointed meeting place.

"Did you see anyone?" Margo whispered.

"No one, and I hope we don't!" Eleanor returned

in a hushed tone. On any other occasion, Margo might have teased her about being a scaredy-cat. For the first time in her life, however, she too felt a real presence of evil: a storm cloud that threatened to engulf each of their families, given the pirates' execution of their scheme. Eleanor's and her duty, she felt, was to investigate the Whale Tooth Inn in hope of making contact with Rupert and uncovering any possible danger to their grandfathers. Had they arrived on the scene a moment sooner, as it turned out, the truth might have been missed and all lost.

"What is it?" Eleanor asked, halting before Margo's out-stretched arm as they approached the way leading up to the inn.

"Shhhh! I think I hear people." Crouching behind a bush along the roadway, the young spies strained to discern the nature of the voices closing in on their position. When the full reality hit, it was too late to make a move; all that remained was the hope of being overlooked in their meager cover of brush.

"See, there it is again!"

"So it is," said Clay. "So that's what you were set a staring at." On the surface, Clay appeared to be in doubt as to the meaning of the flickering light coming from an upper window in the Whale Tooth Inn. Yet he was well apprised of the light's meaning and had been anticipating the signal. All would have gone as planned had Jack succumbed to his usual round of drinking early in the evening ending in the inevitable drunken slumber. Perhaps he'd sensed Clay's mood of expectancy and so determined to forgo the stupefying liquor. As it turned out, his fixation on the lighthouse signal in time led his eye to the flicker of a lesser light—the very light which beckoned from within the upper window to which their eyes were fastened. The meeting was to have been between Clay and his contact alone. But that was all changed, and the two men moved in uneasy union toward their mutual point of destination.

"Are they gone?" Eleanor breathed out in a nervous tone, straining to see the receding figures. Were it not for a moon shadow that enveloped the girls, the question might never have been voiced. Much to her relief, Margo replied in the affirmative. Still the larger question of Rupert's safety and that of their loved ones loomed before them. In a moment, they were out of hiding and headed on toward the suspected meeting place of the pirates. Moving from shadow to shadow along the length of roadway, they crept onward inch-by-inch across the backside of the inn, stopping only when in hearing range of the men's conversation.

"What the blazes! Why didn't you tell me?" Jack snapped.

"I told him not to tell you till I'd made up my mind," the tall stranger replied in Clay's stead; that he and Clay knew to be a lie. Yet he also saw at a glance the relative ease with which Clay's prison-mate could be manipulated.

Jack took in the features of the man standing before him: a large, burly, bullish man of not more than sixty years of age. His slight accent indicated a foreign place of birth. Prison marks were also evident, along with an awkward limp.

"Go on, then," he offered, after the two men had taken stock of each other.

"I don't suppose there's need of my asking whether you told him about the jewels?" the stranger began, looking hard at Clay. "I thought as much," he hunched, guessing at the matter without letting Clay respond. "It looks as though we're in it together then, the three of us. Fair enough! But first we find the gold: that's the plan. Then we set sail for Africa."

Jack looked from the stranger to Clay and back. "What makes you so cocksure it's there?" he questioned, containing his anger whilst picking up on the offer of confidence.

"And just where do you speck it might be? It's there, I say. And not a soul aside them natives knows it."

"Damnation!" Jack cursed, turning on Clay. "What about them inmates?"

"It's like I told you, Jack. Only the jay who went on about the gems, see, he run afoul of the other after their release."

"So he did," the stranger scoffed, bolstering Clay's hand. "Seen it myself with these eyes afore taking holt a the one who done the deed. I pried it from him, sure;

else he'd a got clean off to Africa on the first ship. Won't dare move now, confound him. As to the treasure, the site's fixed right here," he boasted, pressing his massive forehead with a thick finger.

"And here," Clay mimicked, playing along. In fact, a murder had occurred in a back alley. And Clay had sought out the men he'd overheard in the quarry. What he'd failed to notice, however, was that he himself was observed. And the lame convict, after his release and murderous act, soon found him out. They'd be partners in seeking the jewels, the man called Butch promised. Jack could be done in at length, as could Rupert and the others if they caused trouble. It appeared a good plan to Clay, despite the likelihood of Jack's catching on.

"And the map?" Jack insisted, eyeing the men with mistrust, masked behind a show of interest.

"We have no secrets, Jack." The comment from Clay, high-lighted by a crooked smile, provoked only grave silence. It was something about the stranger, more so even than Clay, that made him wary.

"That's it, mate, no secrets!" the stranger parroted.

"Then I'm guessing you'll let me in on the real aim of your meeting tonight. And don't suppose I'm a man to be crossed, I ain't!"

"Jack, I told you we was fixing to bring you in on the plan," Clay gestured, the wear of age and prison evident in his weakened frame.

At this, Jack might have struck the pitiful old bandit to the ground were it not for the stranger. "Am I a dog? What plan? Speak, I tell ya, or I'll… "

"You'll listen, if you've any sense!" the man called Butch rebuffed. Again Jack took measure of the stout figure. Years at sea with ill company had taught him to trust no one. "It's all as he said, we'd a let on before. But here we are and no need waiting."

"I reckon it could be," Jack granted, leaving room for words.

"Could be and is, Jack," said Clay. "And, as you know, part of the plan is set. When them kids show their faces, we grab 'em, case them grandpas of theirs play us for fools."

In an instant, Margo's hand was over Eleanor's mouth, thus preventing the gasp that threatened to hasten the pirates' plan.

Hush! she communicated in silence with a finger to her lips, reinforcing the warning with her eyes.

Jack's face burned in response to Clay's suggestion. "How's that?"

"No matter," Butch asserted. "We've been watched, is all, spied out by a man I saw the night of the murder. Let's just say, I pressed him to show his face here tomorrow night. Let's say, I have him and his sort under my thumb, though they'd as soon see me hanged. Aye, they'll be here, seven o-clock as agreed, or they'll be apt to lose more than gold."

"Damn me! Is that a riddle?"

"Patience, Jack, no call to worry," Clay said. The words, met with a hot stare, were brushed aside by a further query directed at the stranger.

"And the innkeeper?"

"He'll be quiet, I speck. Just follow Clay's lead and keep an eye out for the signal. Two flashes means the birds are in the cage."

"And if they fail to show?"

"Like you put it to them brats, Jack, they'll be wishin' they had, see."

An oppressive air enveloped this remark, the girls shrinking back before the scowling faces they imagined to be bearing down on their covert. Much to their relief, the pirates did not appear. And soon a stark quiet filled the air through which the weary spies made their way homeward.

"Not a word till school's out! Agreed?"

"Agreed!" Eleanor consented, tired from the tense outing yet excited with Margo about the anticipated visit with their grandparents. Were it not for the girls' unwavering faith in these heroes, the feeling might have been one of anxiety mixed with a certain dread. Nonetheless, on the way home they'd decided proper care must be taken. After all, they'd been out past midnight spying on pirates, though not without good reason. Also their report would run counter to Rupert's letter, calling into question his plan. No, it wasn't a simple task they faced, nor was it one in which they'd dare fail. Filled with such thoughts, they climbed the familiar trees nature had place by their bedroom windows and slipped into bed, watched only by the wise old owl that was well familiar with the girls' nocturnal escapades.

Come morning and breakfast, Margo and Eleanor were each surprised by the absence of their grandpas. Nor did their parents or siblings know anything of the matter except for the likelihood of their having gone off fishing. This the girls doubted, given the circumstances. Could it be the elders knew? Struggling with similar doubts, the two friends found it almost impossible to focus on school that day. Would the bell ever ring? Would they find their grandpas in their usual relaxed conversation on one or the other's front porch? At last, the answer came with a resounding *ring… ring… ring* of the school bell and the familiar scene of the two retired sailors. Having run the full length of the way home from school, the girls labored for breath as each relayed the account they'd worked out with care after slipping away from the inn the night before.

"Hold your horses, you two!" Grandpa John appealed, his face a mixture of humor and concern.

"We aren't going anywhere, that's sure," Grandpa Joe noted.

"Oh Grandpa Joe, you must believe us; you must!" Margo pleaded.

"Please, Grandpa John, there's so little time," Eleanor

concurred. Taken aback, the elders looked in wonder at one another and then at their granddaughters.

"Fact is, we've got news for you," Joe began. "In the face of it, however, you two'd best finish your account." At this, Margo began to unfold the entire train of events leading up to the Whale Tooth Inn and the pirate's conversation, which Eleanor then managed to reconstruct in detail, much to Margo's satisfaction. The two elders listened intently, sitting back and stroking their beards.

"You know, Margo, I can't say as your parents will be pleased to hear about your midnight venture." The statement of Grandpa Joe brought an immediate flood of appeals from Margo and Eleanor, who each knew the risk they'd taken in revealing the facts. Even so, it couldn't be helped. And given the circumstances, Joe and John felt the matter better left unmentioned. "We'll let you off the hook on one condition," Joe went on, leaning forward on his knee. "You must promise to stay clear of pirates, inns, and sea caves until this whole ordeal is over and done. Your word, mind!"

"But Grandpa, what will you do?"

"First promise, then we'll add what we know to your own account." Eager to help, the girls consented. Then Joe began, "Though I hate to admit it, given your mischief, your venture has provided a vital clue to our own search."

"You mean, you weren't out fishing this morning?" asked Eleanor, eliciting a low chuckle from the men.

"So everyone supposed, did they?" said John. "It's just as well. And well, too, everyone remains a good way off from them cutthroats. Ay, Joe!"

"It was one of them bandits Rupert chanced to encounter the evening of the murder," Joe began. "As he told us this morning, he was at the Bull's Eye tavern the night of his coming ashore when his eye landed on two men who stood out from the rest. They were ex-convicts, by their looks, and he was minded to keep at a distance, not wanting trouble. To his dismay, one of them came his way and asked if he knew of any ships set to sail for Africa. Used to such questions on account of his sailor's garb and manner, he replied he was not. The man nodded and turned away, only to leave out the back some while later with the other man."

"Acting on impulse," John added, "for reasons he failed to grasp at the time, Rupert went out after the men and watched as they vanished into a dark alley. Hiding himself in the shadows, he overheard a scuffle that soon ended with a muffled cry. Pressed close into a portal, he waited till one of the convicts passed by. Only later was he to learn that he'd been set up by the murderer who threatened slander were Rupert to act."

"Then the pirate with the bad leg lied to the man named Jack about the murder," Margo observed.

"And somehow threatened Rupert were he to tell the real truth," added Eleanor.

"That's so." Grandpa John said. "Knowing himself

to be a visitor in these parts, and seeing the danger of his being unjustly branded a murderer by the rogue, Rupert saw fit to lay low. His plans to see us hindered, he found an old, hollowed-out tree at Spring Creek and hid out."

"The tree!" Eleanor exclaimed.

"Rupert did mention overhearing the pirates while seated in one of the giant cedars of the area," said Margo. "Though he didn't say where."

"No, I speck he didn't," John returned. "Nor did he learn more of the matter till he searched out the camp kept by Clay and Jack not far from the caves. Angered by the rascals' fire setting mischief, he soon found his concern over slander out-weighed by a keen desire to bring all three pirates to justice. But how? That was the question he faced. Later, by chance, he spied out Clay and the stranger who'd murdered the fellow ex-convict. It was clear from their words that the man named Jack was being used in a plot to search out a stash of gold and would soon be dealt with in the same way."

"Sometime later," said Joe, "when Jack and Clay were gone from their camp, Rupert penetrated the sea caves on the hunch of finding further evidence of the pirates' plans; this he uncovered in the form of an old map kept in a box alongside a stockpile of weapons. A day later, he heard the same two men talk of a church picnic they'd got wind of and their hope of laying hold of a further map they somehow suspected to be in my keeping; though how they'd come to this he couldn't say. Nor did he find out their reason for burning down part of Spring Creek till he put the pieces of the puzzle together and grasped their plan."

"To draw the map-holder into the sea caves!" Margo realized with a start.

"So he assumed. Sure enough, as the time drew near, Jack and Clay retreated into the inner part of the caves. It was then Rupert saw fit to stand watch at the entry. And there he prevented your way and so kept the pirates from their desired end," Joe concluded with a feeling of gratitude.

"But Grandpa, why did Rupert give in to the murderer's demand? Why the secretive note?" Margo asked.

"Why did he appear to go along, you mean? The note was a means of keeping us from danger."

"I don't understand," Margo admitted.

"Nor would you, not knowing of our old friendship with Rupert. He assumed, first of all, that we'd take his note as more than a warning. No, his wish for a meeting could mean but one thing: he was in danger, as well as we."

"Also," Grandpa John noted, "he knew we'd question a plan to meet in the evening, though that was the ultimatum given him by the stranger. Rupert's secret message was that we were to arrive in the morning before daybreak. He confirmed our suspicions with the phrase Bonita Santa Maria, for Joe first met Maria when out watching the sunrise, as we all knew, and the phrase had come to be a sort of code word. Further his mention of meeting at our usual place, after alluding to the Whale Tooth, clued us into the real site of our rendezvous: the old lighthouse where we'd all met before in years past."

"Wow," chimed in Eleanor, "that's neat!"

"Maybe so, darling, but there's a good deal more to be done, I'm afraid," her grandpa cautioned.

"You said it," Joe agreed. "And we've a rough road ahead. For the men you two eluded are shrewd as they come. Nor would a charge be like to stand up against them in court, being as any testimony could be thrown out for lack of evidence. Not to mention the stranger's threat of turning Rupert in on false charges, if pressed to do so. No, we're on our own."

"Still there's a bit more to this mystery than first meets the eye," John acknowledged. To this, Joe nodded in agreement, while the girls looked on with incomprehension.

"What do you mean, Grandpa?" Eleanor asked.

"It's about the gold, I'm afraid, and the articles Margo discovered in the early summertime. Well, it wasn't a mere whim that caused her father to visit that part of the country. He'd heard Joe and I talk of the place oft enough and supposed it held features that caught our attention: like the fishing and berry picking. But we never made mention of the cave, nor did we care to bring up the topic. It was rather put out of mind for a number of years. Then of a sudden he took a fancy to see the area. So, by what now appears as more than coincidence, Margo found the entry to our retreat."

"Your retreat!" said Margo.

"It was a chance find, I'll admit," said John.

"I recall the discovery as if it were yesterday," Joe reflected. "We were just returned from sea and our trip to the island monastery. The island we'd found deserted, in keeping with Fernando's account. Nonetheless he took to the place like a man who'd reached home after many a year. It was clear his treasure was the tropical paradise that would thereafter be his residence. Soon he and his crew set to work on the ruins of what had once been the thriving monastery of former days. The crew, we learned, had agreed to a man to join their captain in this new life. Then, too, Fernando wanted us to experience the island as he first had, hoping perhaps we'd pull up anchor for good with the rest. We did stay on to help out for a few months. We might have remained, were it not for a persistent longing that drew us homeward to Witherspoon. Only when Fernando saw that our course was set did he mention the gold. It was there all along, he knew, in the place only he would think to look, there at the spot from which Rodolfo carried him years back during his bout with the ague."

"The treasure was ours for the taking," John

affirmed. "It was of no use to Fernando, as he himself declared, and he liked the idea of its being used for good in America. We'd as soon have left the chest buried where it lay or dumped the coins into the sea, by that time, but he insisted. In our minds, the contrast of the gold and natural beauty of the island could not have been greater. With each waking moment, part of us wished the island would be our final home on earth. But it wasn't to be. Couldn't have you two left without grandparents, now could we?"

"No, Grandpa!" said Eleanor, returning his smile.

"There, you see," Joe said, "the real treasure: the people we care for and love."

"I see what you mean," said Margo. "We've been looking for a treasure that's been here all along."

"But the pirates," Eleanor posed, "will they understand?"

"We can pray so, child. Yet we must be alert. And you two must stay out of trouble, as promised," Grandpa John insisted.

On that note, the voice of Maria called out from across the lane: "Margo, Margo, time to come home!"

Margo was out of her chair and in her grandpa's arms. "Be careful, Grandpa, won't you?"

"Don't mind us! We won't let them foxes get the advantage, ay John!"

"Right you are!" he concurred, reassuring Eleanor with a hug. "Now get along, you two. We'll finish the story of our journey home and use of the mountain cave when the bandits are behind bars or driven off to sea. Would that they'd relent of their mischief. They'll not be harming any of us, in any case, you may be sure."

With that, Margo dashed off homeward while Eleanor went to help her mother. Mealtime in either household failed to witness the elders, who the girls knew to be in pursuit of the men whose sole aim in life appeared to be that of gold and jewels. Meanwhile, life went on as ever in Witherspoon, carrying the girls through the ritual family time, homework, baths, and prayer before bed. Try as they might, neither could sleep on account of their grandpas' failure to return. When the uneasy rest of either friend was interrupted by the *hoot—hoot—hoot* of the curious owl, they could stand it no longer. Suppose their grandpas were in some sort of trouble. Maybe they'd been taken in a trap. Like two detectives focused on the same case, both girls were dressed and out their windows in a minute, ready to stir each other into action and glad to find this unnecessary on spying one another in the moonlight. They were a team, like their grandpas. And they'd see to the safety of these heroes, even if it meant breaking their solemn oath. Thus resolved, they set out into the night.

The Sea Caves

Margo and Eleanor made their way through the moonlight on course to the Whale Tooth Inn, the hoot-owl's call and searching eyes pursuing them as to ask with the town: "Whoooo's creeping along the streets at night? Whoooo? Whoooo? Whooo's into mischief? The twoooo: the twoooo who sneak through the dark of night! That's whoooo! Whooo!" But soon the fear of detection faded with the call of the owl. And the girls, reaching the edge of town, mingled their voices with the cool misty air.

"What do you suppose might have happened?" Eleanor asked, wondering with her friend at the failure of their grandpas to return home.

"I don't know," said Margo. "Maybe the pirates got the better of Rupert. Or maybe they got suspicious and changed their plans, suspecting a trap."

"Still, it doesn't make sense: no word, no news, nothing!"

"I know, I know! We'll just have to wait to find out."

"Margo, what will we do if there's no one there?" The thought hadn't occurred to its recipient, and she hesitated.

"If that's the case, we'll just have to investigate the Mermaid Inn as well."

"And if they're not at the Mermaid?" The girls looked at each other and whispered in unison: "Pirates' Cove!" Why the thought struck them both they couldn't say; it was pure intuition. Thus they weren't surprised to find the Whale Tooth quiet as a tomb. Unnerved by the thought of the pirates' return, the two were on their way out when a muffled cry froze them in place. Fighting off the impulse of flight, they moved with caution toward the source of the voice. It was the innkeeper, bound and gagged and left in the wake of the pirates' departure.

"Finally!" he announced in wide-eyed amazement, rubbing the rope-burn marks on his wrists. He'd scarce recovered his wits when the girls slipped off and passed through the front entry headed out to the Mermaid Inn.

"That was a close one!" said Eleanor. "He might have kept us from our purpose, from the looks of him."

"I had the same feeling. Wonder where he came from? Must be new to these parts. Wonder if he'll stick around, huh Eleanor?"

Eleanor grinned. "Not for long, I'd wager!" The shared humor soon turned to wariness, however, as the girls spied the Mermaid Inn at a distance. Yet they found the inn quiet as the other.

"Strange," Margo said as they moved along the moonlit path toward the cove, "the binding of the innkeeper suggests a trap, yet the absence of the pirates points to a sudden departure, perhaps even the taking of Rupert by force before our grandpas could come to his aid."

"It can't be, Margo! They met with Rupert just yesterday morning."

"I see your point. Then too, it's hard to imagine Rupert walking into a trap, much less our grandpas."

"So how do the pieces fit together?"

"Yeah, how?" The two walked on together in silence, the lull of crickets sounding in their ears. "I've got it!" Margo said of a sudden, turning to her friend. "A second map! There must be a second map to the treasure!"

"Second map?"

"Sure! Remember Grandpa Joe's words about the real treasure being the people we care for and love?"

"Well?"

"Mightn't it follow then that to protect us our

grandpas could have offered up the gold in exchange for the pirates' departure?"

"Could be, I suppose. But what do you mean second map?"

"I mean, it's possible our grandpas had a second or duplicate map in case the one sealed up in the mountain cave were to be lost or stolen."

"I see your point."

"Course, hidden as it was, and the cave's entry being so narrow and all, that wasn't likely to happen. In any case, if there were a second map, they could have given it to the pirates and then laid up in waiting to make sure they kept their end of the bargain."

"Then where is the treasure?"

"Where else? In the sea caves, where it's always been, and in a place the pirates failed to look."

"But how can we be sure, Margo?"

"Simple! The mountain cave is too open—too obvious and accessible. It's almost as if Grandpa Joe expected it to be discovered in time and so dropped suggestive hints to my father, though he missed the meaning of the clues. Surely that sanctuary was meant for a place of retreat."

"Like the island, yet it's ruled out too!" Eleanor reasoned, picking up on the train of her friend's logic.

"And Pirates' Cove with its sunken vessel! Which leaves?"

"The sea caves!" they exclaimed in unison. All this

while, they'd been keeping a watchful eye and open ear as they moved on toward the cove and caves beyond. They'd hoped to come across the camp of their grandpas and Rupert along the way, but no camp was to be seen.

"Maybe we're wrong, Margo. Maybe there is another hiding place. Or maybe the pirates have gone off by now with the treasure." It was true; they could have erred in their analysis. The thought of being on a wild goose chase made this possibility even harder to swallow. All the same there was nothing for it but to go on in hope of solving the mystery.

"Look!" The abrupt directive coupled with Eleanor's out-stretched arm and pointing finger dispelled the cloud of doubt. There, just visible in the distance, the faint glimmer of two lights marked what the girls recognized to be the main entry to the sea caves.

"I knew it," Margo announced, proud of the achievement.

"What do we do now?"

"Go forward, what else?" Were it not for the uncertain state of their grandparents, Eleanor might have balked at the proposal. As it was, she steeled her will along with Margo and advanced by her friend's side into the open area where moonlight, sea, and torch-lit portal converged in eerie union. Little did they realize that at the moment of their departure from the forested path an undetected watchman was turning his eyes from the scene in response to his relief. Ready to risk their lives on behalf of those they loved, the girls lifted the flaming torches from their metal holders on either side of the cave's entry and together penetrated the darkness of the forbidden labyrinth.

"No sign, Joe?"

"None. Don't know what to make of it. They've been in those caves a good stretch; should have reached the spot by now."

"Looks like we'll just have to wait. There's but one land-side entry, and few would dare brave the sea entry at high tide, much less low."

"That's so, John. I'd best get some rest. We'll listen for the call."

"Right!" said John, moving ahead to the lookout spot. The call was not long in coming. And soon the three men stood gazing down in wonder at the darkened cave entrance below.

"What the blazes! How in the world?"

"But there it is, Joe!"

"Confound the luck!" said Rupert.

"Escape in haste with that load? Besides, I checked the path, not a trace of light to be seen." Silence fell on the men as they considered the case. There was but one explanation: an insight neither John nor Joe were inclined to allow.

John shook his head. "It ain't luck."

"It can't be!" Joe shifted, meeting the anxious look of his friend.

"I'm afraid we've no choice but to find out," John replied.

"What's your meaning?" Rupert asked.

"Our granddaughters, Margo and Eleanor. It would be just like them to trail us out of concern. I should have thought."

"Won't do our fretting now, Joe. We've no time to waste." John's assertion was met with nods of unison. Soon the men were pressing into the darkness of the caves in search of the girls, who by this time were nearing the first major opening indicated on the map. For most, a step-by-step use of the map would have been needful. For Margo, who'd spent hours fixing every detail of the drawing in her mind, the cave was as a familiar pattern that could just as well be walked blindfolded. She's made a point of noting the danger spots where, to the girls' dismay, they passed the skeletal remains of those whose fate it was to become part of the sea caves lore."

"It can't be much further," Margo whispered.

"Wait!" Eleanor motioned, her heart skipping a beat. "What's that?" The girls stopped to listen, hearing what seemed to be faint voices coming from opposite directions.

"I don't know. Come on, let's keep moving."

"Margo, the torches! What if we're spotted?"

"We'll have to risk it. Only we must be quiet." Taking the hint, Eleanor moved on in doubt, images of one-eyed, scar-faced pirates with brandished swords filling her imagination.

"One more step and you're dead where you stand!" The coarse voice of Clay pierced the cavern and sent shivers of fear through the alarmed frames of the unsuspecting pair. A moment later the contorted face and menacing figure of the pirate emerged some twenty feet beyond the girls' position. To turn and flee would be futile, as the twin muskets pointing their way indicated. All seemed lost. Coming closer, the old bandit let out a gruff laugh. "So, got past the lookouts, I see. Don't that beat all! Just or luck! Fine, we'll have no trouble with you two in tow. Sure as you must of seen our need," he added with a wry smile. "Now, get along, ya hear! And don't go acting up!"

"Oh no you don't, Clay!" the commanding thrust of Joe's voice threatened. "You've got your part of the deal. Now let the girls go!"

"Grandpa!" Margo cried out across the opening, the second broad expanse through which they'd only just passed prior to being abducted. There was no getting around Clay, however, who held the girls at bay while looking hard at the three men.

"Kept your part, eh? Don't look so to this sailor. How do ya 'count for them two?"

"There's one of you and three of us, Clay!" John pressed. "Best let them go, if you know what's good for you!" It was so, Clay perceived. And the five torches round about, including those of the girls, reinforced the fact.

"Not so fast!" The voice of Jack, trailed by the ominous figure of Butch, frustrated the men's purpose and restored in Clay an air of confidence. "It appears we hold the cards, after all. Do ya take us for fools, to drop our prey on sight a your ugly faces?"

"You're under oath, Jack," Rupert countered. "Give up the girls, and we'll be on our way."

At this, Jack broke into a mocking laugh. "Sure as you call up a time when the gold was good as mine. That's it, Joe! You follow, like you do the slash you made on this here face. Curse that liver-bellied captain! Curse him! Now it looks to be my turn. Twenty long years I waited for this!"

"You and me, then, and none other!" Joe readied, seeing no way round the challenge. At that, Jack lurched forward like a man possessed, bent on the vengeance he'd sworn with every reminder of the scar that marked him for life. The stranger, casting a dark eye at Joe, looked on with indifference, not caring which of the men fell.

"Grandpa!" Margo cried out again, only to be stilled by a move of Joe's hand and look of assurance. None but John and Rupert could have anticipated the skill with which he'd prove master of his rival. In minutes the fight was over, Jack face down to the ground, his knife laid out at a distance.

"End it!" said Clay.

"End it, why don't you?" said Jack. Given the chance, he'd fight on, this he and Joe knew.

"Damn the coward!" the stranger cursed, glaring at Joe with an air of defiance. "If you'll not, I will!" Even as the villain drew his sword, John's voice rumbled through the cavern and out along the entryways. Throwing himself forward before the stranger could advance, he stood in fierce defiance of the assassin, aiming an accusatory finger.

"The devil you will! You! The one who filled our heads with the promise of jewels then butchered our mates at them bloody falls! Tarnation! Lying traitor! What say we have a trial of our own, seeing you've the nerve to show you face in these parts. You a judge? I'd sooner be hanged!"

Cut by the words, the man named Butch advanced on his accuser with the aim of doing what he'd failed at years back. Tossing John a sword, Rupert watched with concern as Joe and Jack gave way and the two men laid into each other. Had it been another moment, another day, another rival, John might have reeled back under strain of the attack. He was outmatched by the man who stood a full six-inches taller and weighed some fifty pounds more. Yet the furry ignited by the thought of the fiend, come as he had to place Eleanor in danger, was such as no force on earth could withstand. Blow after blow, he bettered his foe, seizing the advantage of his bad leg and driving him back time and again. The battle was intense and none could be sure its outcome, till the steely resolve of John worked the sword from the stranger's grasp and came near to striking him down.

"No, John!" Joe cried out, preventing the sweep of the sword. Brought to his senses, John motioned his antagonist to the side of Jack, who sat under Joe's guard.

"The game's up, Clay!" Rupert urged, compelling the last bandit to face reality.

"You'll not take me alive!" he swore, raising a pistol in John's direction. At the same instant in a rush of adrenalin, acting out of pure emotion and protective fear, Eleanor drove her torch into the pirate's back, causing the bullet to miss its mark and ricochet off the cavern wall. Margo was quick to follow, knocking the other pistol from Clay's left hand and driving him to his knees in the face of the burning flames. All eyes were fixed on Clay, thus none but Jack noticed the slumped figure of the man called Butch, and this only after Clay was subdued. He was dead: shot through the temple with the bullet from Clay's pistol. It was over, and nothing remained but to lead the two captives out, leaving the body of the slain pirate behind with the coins he'd coveted.

At one-o-clock the following day, Margo and Eleanor awoke to the whistle of the local ferryboat that made runs to and from the nearby island. Grandpas

Joe and John had managed to carry the sleepy girls to their beds the night before without disturbing either household. Come morning, they'd explained the night's events to the girls' parents before setting off to meet up with Rupert. Hence, much to their surprise, the young heroes received hugs and kisses from their parents. There'd be no more midnight outings, that was made plain. And they were to stay clear of the sea caves and also of pirates.

"But mom, we were just trying to help Grandpas Joe and John."

"No buts, Margo! Now run along and play. I'm sure you and Eleanor have lots to talk about. Just be glad your father and I have agreed with her parents to let you two off the hook this time. Oh, and by the way, Grandpa Joe says he and John will be back around suppertime, so don't be late."

"Yes, mother!" The words trailed in the air behind the elated figure of Margo as she flew through the front door on course to Eleanor's house.

"That girl!" Maria mused, feeling the joy of her daughter's freedom while reflecting on her own experiences growing up in Witherspoon.

"Eleanor, Eleanor!" Margo called as she approached her friend's front yard in a rush of exuberance. The object of her enthusiasm, she noticed, was perched on the porch-swing reading a book. Slowing to a walk, Margo realized her friend wasn't looking up. Easing into a chair, she began to sense a feeling of release she herself had managed, unlike Eleanor, to repress. Perhaps it was the look on Eleanor's face. In any case, she soon came to appreciate the silence. It was, for all they knew, a work of nature meant to heal the heart of trauma: anguish the conscious mind was unable to bear. Tears began to flow from the eyes of both girls as they felt the full impact of what they'd endured. It was a happy cry. And soon they were off to the bay to swim and play with the other children, to build elaborate sandcastles and put behind them the trauma of death and treachery that for a time threatened their world.

The Trial

The trial of Jack and Clay was set for Wednesday afternoon. Much to their parents' dismay, Margo and Eleanor were called upon as witnesses.

"Look at all the people!" Margo marveled aloud.

"Guess the County Fair wasn't excitement enough for one year!" Eleanor joked.

"Guess not," said Margo, a whimsical look on her face. The carefree spirit of play common to the two was soon dampened when a hush announced the arrival of the men who were to stand trial. After Clay and Jack had taken their seats, a loud *bang, bang, bang* echoed throughout the chamber, causing the girls' hearts to jump even as their eyes met those of the pirates.

"Court is now in session!" The judge, a powerful figure with jet-black hair and piercing eyes, motioned the prosecution to call the first witness.

"If it pleases the court, I call Joseph Whitaker to the stand." Mounting the steps to place his right hand on the Bible, Joe swore to tell the truth before God and took his seat.

Pointing to the accused, the prosecutor asked, "Do you recognize these men?"

"I do."

"Can you tell the court where they were last Friday night, the time of the shooting and their arrest?"

"I can. They were down in the sea caves looking for gold."

"And how was it you knew of their whereabouts?"

"Well sir, that'll take some telling." A low murmur ran through the courtroom in the train of this remark, stifled by a quick rapping of the judge's gavel.

"Go on," the prosecutor, a direct man named Martin encouraged.

"Objection!" All eyes turned to the defense attorney. "Surely a simple answer is all that's required."

"Objection overruled! The background history may prove relevant to the case. You may continue, Mr. Whitaker."

"As I said, it's a bit of a story." At that, Joe recounted his knowledge of Jack and Clay, with emphasis on events leading up to the climactic standoff in the cavern. One might have heard a pin drop during his riveting description of their entry into the caves in hope of saving their granddaughters. When the final scene was depicted, culminating with the shot that found its hapless mark in the man called Butch, a collective gasp filled the courtroom and caused all present to glance at the two accused men.

"Objection, your honor! The witness is stating as fact that which has yet to be proved."

"Objection overruled," the judge declared, motioning the prosecution to proceed.

"No further questions, your honor."

"You say the pistol was aimed at Mr. Stanley from a close range. Is that correct?" the defense attorney began.

"That's how it was."

"And from your testimony you indicate the accused was an accurate shot?"

"So I've been told, but…"

"But you say his aim was thrown off by the girls seated in the witness area."

"Yes, but…"

"Then how do you know the pistols weren't meant to serve as a mere warning?"

"Objection! Your honor, the reality of murder is at issue here, not the supposed motive of the accused."

"Objection overruled! Continue."

"I know, sure as I've eyes to see. No, it wasn't a warning, by God. It was a shot meant to take John down, and we'd a been next, were it not for the girls."

"Yet you said the girls were behind the accused. How then can you be certain as to who acted first?"

"It was plain to everyone. And they did what was right, what any child might do to protect a loved one."

"No further questions!" With that, Joe left the stand, feeling a bit uneasy about the final exchange.

"The defense will call its next witness."

"Your honor, I call Margo Whitaker to the stand."

Taking a deep breath, Margo moved in measured steps toward the front, her eyes fixed on the chair so as to avoid contact with the pirates who sat in an enclosed area off to the left of the swearing-in place.

"Do you, Margo Whitaker, swear to tell the truth, the whole truth, and nothing but the truth, so help you God?"

"Yes sir," she replied, plucking up courage to take the stand.

"Can you tell the people here today why you were in the sea caves on the night of the accident?"

"Objection! Do we know that the shooting was accidental?"

"Sustained. You will re-phrase the question, Mr. Piper."

"On the night of the shooting, you were present and held in check by one of the defendants prior to the appearance of your grandfather and his companions. Why?"

"It wasn't our fault, sir. We were just trying to help our grandpas." A ripple of laughter punctuated this remark.

"The court will please remain silent during the proceedings," Judge Thornton announced, laying aside his gavel.

"And what made you think they'd be in the sea caves in the middle of the night?"

Looking over at Eleanor and back at the man before her she said, "We just sort of guessed at it." Another flurry of muffled laughter, stifled by the judge's gavel, enlivened the chamber.

"Was it often their habit to visit the sea caves at such an hour?"

"Objection! Your honor, the supposed habits of witnesses can have no bearing on the case."

"Objection sustained."

"Was there any reason for your grandfather to be where you thought you'd find him after midnight as it was?"

Margo looked at her grandpa, who gave her a nod of reassurance. "Yes, sir, we knew our grandpas were onto the pirates. And we figured the pirates might be hid out in the caves."

"How did you know all this? Can you tell the court?"

"Well, sir, it all sort of got started back in the summer." So Margo began, rehearsing the main details of the odd string of events leading up to the sea cave standoff, though she managed to avoid mention of the mountain sanctuary's location.

"Then you admit your grandfather and his companions knew of the gold's presence in the caves?" Again Margo looked at her grandfather and then back.

"Y-yes, sir, but it's not like you're thinking."

"Thank you, your honor. No more questions." The response, cutting short Margo's explanation, made her wish all the more to be out of the public eye and in her seat.

Noting her distress, the prosecution rose. "Nothing for the present, your honor."

"You may step down, young lady," the judge directed. Feeling she might have said something wrong, Margo made an uneasy pathway to her place in the witness area. And while her grandpa exuded quiet confidence, she had a new and peculiar sense of his vulnerability. "Next witness, Mr. Martin!"

"Your honor, if it please the court, I call upon one of the accused who goes by the name of Jack." Little could Joe or anyone else in the witness area guess at the thoughts that had troubled the ex-convict ever since his lost fight in the cavern. Much as he tried to deny it, his old spirit of anger had been broken and a new brooding had taken its place.

Why'd he do it? he thought again, as he walked to the witness stand and mumbled a response to the swearing-in ceremony.

"I'd like to ask you a few simple questions," Martin began. "Were you or were you not present when the two girls were taken captive by Clay?"

"Objection! The charge of abduction is yet to be proved!"

"Sustained! Mr. Martin, if you please?"

"Were you present when the two girls were held at bay by Clay?"

"Absent, I were, but for the talk that come our way."

"You mean to say, you and the deceased man?"

"That's it!"

"And the three men seated here before you, when did they appear on the scene, and what were they after?" Joe steadied himself for the response, but was surprised by the answer given.

"They came up, all right, 'bout the time we was drawing nigh to Clay."

"Go on," Martin prompted, noting Jack's awkwardness, as did Clay with growing mistrust.

"It was a standoff, sure, and they was set on them girls." Again he paused. "See here, I done my time—twenty long years! No, I weren't looking to hurt no kids. But see here!" he insisted, pointing to the scar-line across his face. "It was vengeance I wanted, that I swore with every drive of the wedge in that cursed quarry: vengeance on the man that cut me down!" A puzzled look in Joe's direction accompanied a further hesitation. "Damn the man! Why didn't he end it? Why?"

"Objection! Your honor, I fail to see the relevance of the testimony given."

"Overruled!"

Picking up on the judge's nod, Jack continued. "It was him or me, and we knew it was life or death. So he should 'ave done me, confound it!"

"Is that all?" This follow-up had the effect of turning Jack's head in the direction of Clay, who met his burning gaze with cautious defiance.

"All? Aye, it would a been, if that dead dog had his way. I see it now, the cur!" The statement, though enigmatic to the general public, caused Joe to lean forward and take stock of the man set before him.

"That's all, your honor," Martin concluded, preventing the objection he knew would be forthcoming.

"Counsel for the defense forgoes cross-examination at this time," Piper conceded, suspecting his rival had somehow gained access to Jack prior to the trial, though how he couldn't say. "I call on Mr. John Stanley," he continued when Jack was seated. Eleanor felt her heart skip on hearing her grandfather's name. Within moments he was facing the defense counsel.

"Mr. Stanley, were you cognizant of the map used by my clients to locate the gold?"

"I was. And we'd have given it to them well and again if we thought it would safeguard our families."

"And where did you first come by this map?"

Hesitating, John said at length, "That's rather involved, if you really want to know."

"Objection! The line of inquiry is leading us far from the subject of concern."

"Overruled! Continue, Mr. Piper."

"Thank you, your honor. Mr. Stanley, if you'd start from the beginning."

"I suppose you could say it all began when Joe found the first map during a stop in Spain." On he went through the halls of memory to the miraculous rescue at the hand of Fernando and his crew to the island and its buried treasure.

"And this treasure," Piper asserted, interrupting the narrative, "you spirited away to its secretive place of hiding within the sea caves! Is that not the case, Mr. Stanley?"

"If you wish to put it that way. But it's not as you may suppose."

"And what should one suppose, given the circumstances?"

"Objection! Your honor, I would ask the defense counsel to refrain from the present line of questioning. Mr. Stanley is not on trial here."

"Objection sustained. Mr. Piper, you will please take a new approach."

"Mr. Stanley," Piper began afresh, undaunted by the objection, "are you prepared to prove your rightful claim to the treasure?"

"I'm not sure as to what you mean."

"I mean, do you possess papers indicating your rightful and legal ownership of the gold?"

"Papers? The subject never came up. It was Fernando's right to use the gold however he chose."

"And we're to believe he chose to give the fortune to you and Mr. Whitaker? Is that your meaning?"

"It is, though we cared nothing for it after all we'd endured. Our only thought was to reach America and our loved ones. The gold was Fernando's idea."

"And the caves? I suppose that was his idea too?"

"No, sir, not at first." A pause accentuated this elusive remark, a hesitation understood by only one other person in the room.

"Where then did you put the gold at first? And why wasn't it reported to the proper authorities?"

Again the strained silence, and then, "I can't say; I'd be breaking a solemn oath, which no true sailor would ever do."

"Then you refuse to explain the reason behind your actions?"

"On my word, we've acted in good faith, but I can't break my oath, not for you or any man." At this, Piper focused in like a hound on its prey.

"Your honor, it has come to my attention that the gold in question once belonged to a Spanish nobleman who on departing this world left the vast sum to the state. As the report rumored abroad and documented in the government files on the case indicates, the treasure was transported from Spain by unknown means and hidden on a certain island in the Caribbean. From this island one of my clients fled, only to be taken into custody off this very shore. He has since paid for his crimes and now stands falsely accused by the real bandits: Joe Whitaker and John Stanley!"

"Objection! Objection!" The outcry of Martin was soon accompanied by a general outbreak of chatter throughout the courtroom.

"I yield the floor," Piper added in response to a loud hammering of the gavel marking off his steps.

"Order! Order in the court!" the judge thundered, bringing the noise to a hush. "I would remind you, Mr. Piper, that the accusations you propose are of a serious nature and will need to be proved beyond a reasonable doubt. You may proceed with the cross-examination, Mr. Martin."

Seeing the uncertain state of his client, Martin replied, "Your honor, I request a recess from the present proceedings for a space of twenty-four hours."

"Under the circumstances, such a recess would be welcome. This court will reconvene at four-o-clock tomorrow afternoon!"

A cool breeze struck the faces and hands of two men as they grasped the iron bars of their prison cells and gazed out across a turbulent sea. Witherspoon Jail was situated to the north of town on a hillside overlooking the coastline and ocean beyond. Little used over the years, it served mostly as a drying out place for drunks and, on occasion, a temporary holding cell for criminals soon to be moved on to the county or state prisons. The two occupants who searched the horizon were, however, unlike any these solitary chambers had witnessed before. They were, in a word, an anomaly in the eyes of the jailor, judge, general public, and prosecuting attorney, the latter of which having failed in the coarse of two further court hearings to overcome the devastating effect of the defense counsel's surprise accusations.

Piper himself had enjoyed the final word on the subject of the map, gold, and question of wrongdoing on the part of his clients. Rogues though they were, he was trained to defend even the worst offenders, whether they be innocent or guilty, and he'd done so to perfection, turning the increasingly suspicious mindset of the jury members away from the accused to certain members of the witness area who'd confessed to a prolonged focus on finding the gold. It was an open and shut case of libel, Piper concluded, much to the amazement and dismay of Joe and John. Yet there was nothing to prevent a further tightening of the noose that Clay had managed to place about his opponents' necks with the studied help of his legal aid.

The fourth and final stage of the trial was set for the third Saturday of November, after an eight-week stay of judgment granted on the part of Judge Thornton in response to the prosecuting counsel's request and in view of the extraordinary nature of the case. Mr. Martin had, at the close of the third session, appealed for an extension on grounds of needing sufficient time to pursue and counter the allegations put forth by Piper. Documents regarding the Spanish municipal government's claim to the gold had to be found and examined. And accusations set forth by Clay, including the charge of libel, needed to be researched. So the stay was granted, but on condition that Joseph Whitaker and John Stanley remain in custody until such time as the full airing of facts might prove to exonerate them.

Piper, having noticed Jack's disturbance of conscience and ill relations with Clay, was careful to minimize his inclusion in the trial, putting more weight on Clay's testimony and on his having aimed his pistols merely in self-defense. He'd further led the court to suspect the girls of being responsible for Clay's pulling of the trigger, as they'd admitted to throwing him off balance in hope of protecting their grandfathers. In the end, though Clay hadn't been liberated of guilt in the eyes of the jury, the initial case was turned on its head and the final verdict left up in the air on account of the stay issued by Judge Thornton.

"Eleanor," Margo began one day, midway through the waiting period, "I've been thinking."

"About what?" The reply, coming out of Eleanor's shared sense of melancholy, was subdued.

"About our approach to the present trial facing Grandpas Joe and John."

"What do you mean?"

"I mean our whole attitude has been one of defeat instead of our having faith."

"How can we have faith at a time like this, Margo?"

"It's not the time, Eleanor, it's the attitude. We've not trusted our need to God."

"I suppose, you're right. But do you think God can do anything to help our grandpas? After all, everything seems to be going against them."

"I know, I know! Yet we must believe; it's our only hope. I've thought of everything—everything, Eleanor! And it's no use. The more I think, the more I seem to see no way out."

"Yeah, I know what you mean."

"So, when you can't see your way out of a problem, look up, as Pastor Donny says."

"You think I haven't prayed? And still our grandpas are in jail."

"Have we really prayed? I mean, really tried to make contact with God?"

"What are you getting at?"

"A prayer retreat, that's what! An escape to the special place where our grandpas used to go."

"The mountain sanctuary?"

"Precisely!"

"Are you mad? Just to get there would take a good three days on foot! What about school and our parents?"

"Eleanor, our grandparents' freedom is at stake! Will anyone fault us for taking a week or so off to ask God for help?"

"A week!"

"Sure! We'll take our grandpas' horses and make it there in a day. Then we stay long enough to get everyone's attention. Get my meaning?"

"I don't know. Sounds like another crazy plan to me."

"Got any better ideas, smarty?"

"N-not exactly!"

"Good, then it's settled!"

"And just how are we to survive out there?"

"Simple! We'll plan on leaving the first day of harvest festival. You know how it is every year: tons of food and all the grownups distracted for three days. Even our families will attend, as our folks said, so as not to appear defeated or without confidence of victory in court."

"You mean, we'll take food from the festival?"

"No, silly! We'll make a list and start laying aside a little at a time what we'll need, that way it won't be missed. Meanwhile, we can make other preparations."

"Right, like blankets, utensils, and other items," said Eleanor, the light beginning to spread over her face.

"We'll get started right away! What do you say?"

"I'm in!" Eleanor smiled, rising to shake Margo's hand.

The Runaways

Before they knew it, the days of preparation had passed and the harvest festival drew near. All was in readiness, and none suspected the scheme that would turn the entire community inside out and cause many to reassess their suspicions of Joe and John. As for the girls, they went about their plan with focused determination, sensing the importance of its success. The final steps went without a hitch as they made their escape from the crowd the morning of the second day and were well on their way to Lookout Mountain by late afternoon. No one noticed the girls' absence till the evening, at which time a general search was made prior to the alarm being sounded at the local police station.

"There's no use our setting out tonight," the sheriff told the eager crew of volunteers. "We'll have to wait till first light, then we head off in five directions, two groups covering the coast and three groups fanning out across the countryside inland. They could be anywhere, men, near or far, and knowing the stress those kids have been under, I suggest we do our best to find them before nightfall tomorrow."

Come the next evening, however, no word arrived regarding the girls' whereabouts. Soon the call went out to neighboring communities for help. Little did the scouting party searching Lookout Mountain realize how close they were to the runaways. Nor did they discover the culvert in which the girls had stabled their horses. As it were, everyone in the region remained on alert in hope of the girls appearance, everyone that is but the girls themselves, who were experiencing a third day of adventure on the mountain and in the rugged sanctuary where Joe and John had spent many a like retreat. At Margo's insistence, they'd seen fit to carry along Grandpa Joe's rifle; it would serve them well, she knew, if any critters got to prowling about.

Meanwhile, the men confined in Witherspoon Jail waited in expectation of the coming trial. Unaware of the girls' plight, the minds of Joe and John were preoccupied with another concern. For unknown to all but themselves, Rupert had set sail on course to the Caribbean not long after their internment. Though they tried to dissuade him, his mind was set and purpose fixed on reaching the Monastery of Santa Maria in hope of procuring help from Fernando. It would take a miracle, they felt, for him to reach the island and return in time to give aid in the conclusive court hearing. First he must locate a ship and captain willing to take on the voyage. Then they'd need to locate the island that many maps excluded. Further he must find Fernando himself, were he yet alive, and persuade him to come. Finally favorable winds would be essential to a swift journey to and from the island. All this! And still the idea of such support making a difference in the trial's outcome brought only doubt to the minds of the prisoners whose faith was fading with the passing of time.

Yet a silver lining remained around an otherwise dark cloud. Joe's cell, as chance and a careless jailor would have it, was set square up against that of Jack, the other two men being kept in a separate section of the prison. At first, the only sounds to be heard were those of nature, or the jail-keeper carrying food in and out, or the pacing of feet within the confined spaces. Then a peculiar event occurred a week or so into the waiting period.

"Why'd ya do it?" The appeal was met with silence, Joe being uncertain as to a reply. Then again, "Why'd ya do it, I say?"

"It was my choice, is all."

"What do ya mean?"

"I'm not the man I was years back when the law of survival ruled my will."

"It don't figure! You could a killed me. You should 'ave, confound it! Why didn't ya?"

"What good would come of your death, Jack?"

"But your face—your pride!"

"So I showed mercy: I spared your life."

"I can't figure it. Something's took my anger. My want of vengeance is gone! Gone, I say! It'll drive me made, do ya hear, if you don't tell me why!"

"It's the Lord, Jack, don't you know? God is dealing with your heart, just as He done me years ago when I turned from that old life."

A long silence followed this remark and remained for the space of three hours. It would be days before Jack's resistance broke and he came to see the futility of fighting God's will. By the fourth week he was a new man, and a surprising friendship began to take shape between cell number's one and two, an occurrence neither man would have dreamed possible. The inner scar was healed and new hope discovered.

The seventh week of Joe and John's prison stay drew to a close, and no sign of the girls was evident. Thus the fathers continued to search with the other men while the women paid visits to the mothers during the hard period of waiting. In spite of everyone's growing fears, however, Maria felt her child to be in good care and free of harm. And though her reason battled with this sense of calm, she was joined by Eleanor's mother, who had a similar sense of peace. A like feeling was shared by their daughters who, amid the sixth day in their mountain retreat, were experiencing the divine presence of God and power of nature as never before.

"Let's sing! Let's sing, Eleanor, like we do at church meetings." So they began to sing, their song filling the space in which they sat and echoing out along the entry corridor. Before long it grew into a beautiful offering of praise and thanksgiving to God for the desired deliverance of their grandparents.

"Oh Margo, I'm so happy, I could sprout wings and fly—fly—fly up to heaven!" The girls were radiant with joy as they circled the cavern over and over again, arms outstretched and hearts light as feathers. In the midst of their dance, Eleanor's eye caught the faint outline of what looked to be a rectangular shape etched into one side of a crevice running on an angle to the cave's northern end. Slowing to a stop, she looked at the outlined shape and then beckoned to her friend.

"Do you see it?"

"See what?"

"The pattern in the wall." Soon the two were at the wall's surface examining the outline with excitement. It was the work of Grandpas Joe and John, they felt, and so were all the more eager to move what proved to be an overlaid stone from its setting. It would take the good part of two hours to do so, working with what tools they had and resting as needed. When the stone was finally moved from its place, the girls discovered a second chest, half the size of the first and fastened with a similar lock, yet no key was to be found.

"Key!" Margo exclaimed. "The second key, of course, I'd almost forgotten."

"You mean, the smaller of the two keys you found here at the first, the one in the chest with the Bible?"

"Yes, Eleanor! But it's not here, it's in the secret hiding place behind the maple tree in my backyard."

"That figures! Oh well, guess we'll just have to wait."

"Yeah, till tomorrow when we'll both catch it from everyone!"

"It's funny, but I'm not worried about our grandpas anymore. Do you feel the same?"

Margo smiled at her friend as she set the chest at the edge of the stone bench nearest the cavern's exit. "I know; it's as if everything's changed. I'm concerned, but not in the same way. We've prayed, and God's answered our prayers in more ways than one, it seems."

"We've found the real treasure!" Eleanor agreed, returning Margo's smile.

"And now, there's nothing to do but pack up and head back with confidence in God's power to deliver them both."

"And us!" Eleanor said with a laugh.

The girls reached Witherspoon the next evening, to the amazement and relief of the entire town. Thus instead of being punished, they were met with pats on the back and sighs on account of their deliverance. Even the men-folk took pride in a job well done. After all, the girls were home safe and sound, and no harm had come to either. So what looked a tragedy was turned into celebration, all but the girls feeling proud of the part they'd played in the ordeal. People would sleep well that night, ignorant of the real change come over the two young-uns. Come morning, the girls managed to give a simple account of their adventure to either sets of parents, including the joy and peace they'd experienced in the mountain sanctuary. They'd all been through a difficult time of testing during the weeks past, the grown-ups realized. It was time to reaffirm their trust in providence as they waited in hope of a just ending to the conclusive trial.

"All hands on deck!" The insistent voice of the captain rang through the lower quarters, stirring the crew to action. He'd not asked payment for the trip; it was a favor given an old friend and shipmate from past voyages. Rupert had recognized James, better known by his men as Captain Clark, on searching out the port for a ship. The latter had just finished unloading what was to be his last shipment of goods when Rupert came aboard. Many years had come and gone since their days of sailing together. Nonetheless, the spirit of camaraderie was strong as ever, and the two men enjoyed a merry session of reminiscing before the need of aid was brought up.

Clark was familiar with Joe and John and listened with growing interest to Rupert's account of the trial and false charges the men had been forced to endure. He was also aware of Clay, the pirate captain having been responsible for a thwarted attack that left a good friend and fellow sailor dead. Fate, it appeared, had presented Clark with the opportunity of helping to bring the ruthless bandit to justice. Retirement would wait out one last trip, he assented, shaking Rupert's grateful hand. A trade stop could be arranged to justify the journey to the crew. Thus plans were set and sails raised in hope of locating the island monastery.

"All hands on deck!" Clark's voice sounded out again as the wind velocity increased and with it the threat of storm. To Rupert's relief, the Caribbean island had been found by the captain and a warm welcome extended the crew. Fernando, the sage leader of the monastery, had taken in the sobering details of the court case and consequent internment. No further persuasion was necessary. He and two other brethren would join with the crew straightway for the return trip. A day and night of smooth sailing had followed prior to the captain's stirring alarm.

"Bosun, make ready for a gale. Could be a bad one, by the looks of it!"

"Aye, aye, Cap'an!"

"Rupert, you'd best see our guests to their cabins. Might get rough up here, and I'll not have any overboard."

"Very good, Captain!" Rupert nodded, knowing the request would be taken in the right spirit by those who were all too well used to the sea from past ventures. To a man, they honored the order. How often Fernando had commandeered his own vessel in foul weather. A worse storm threatened to disrupt the lives of his relatives in Witherspoon, however; and he'd not rest easy till this threat was removed, nor cease in prayer on behalf of those in need. Meanwhile on deck, Clark continued to brace for a storm, yet to his amazement, the wind reached a set intensity and there remained. Moreover, the prevailing wind was favorable to their course, assuring arrival a day in advance of the trial. Thus he was forced to admit that he'd never again underestimate the power of prayer, an acknowledgment well received by Fernando.

All the same, one day would be little time to prepare for the final court battle. Taking up lodgings at the Swan Inn, the men discussed their options in anticipation of every possible legal scenario. They decided it best to observe the court proceedings and to act on their friends' behalf only if necessary, being as the trial might turn in their favor, though that was doubtful.

Elsewhere in the sleepy town of Witherspoon other plans were afoot, empty beds betraying the absence of tree-climbers who looked for each other in the dark.

"Margo! Margo!"

"Shhhh! Not so loud!"

"Sorry. Are you ready?"

"Of course, I'm ready! Come on, let's go!"

Once again, the two companions crept off beneath the round eyes of the curious and secretive owl. The challenge they faced was easy enough: retrieve the chest they'd seen fit to hide on their way back from Lookout Mountain and see if its contents might be of some use to their grandpas, though how they couldn't imagine. Nor could either say why they'd felt inclined to keep the box a secret. How often during the days past they'd wanted to get away. As it turned out, the midnight outing came a mere twelve hours before the set court-hearing time. Traversing the moonlit terrain, the girls moved with unity of purpose, eager to unlock the mystery preserved in the chest.

"Here it is!" said Margo.

"Just as we left it!"

"Only let's hope we're right about the key."

"We have to be! We must be!" Perhaps Eleanor felt the words necessary to success. Or perhaps she'd come to believe that without faith all would be lost. After all, was not faith the force that led to the discovery in the mountain grotto? Surely, it was! And so in the same spirit she looked on, as Margo wedded key to keyhole, closed her eyes and turned her hand and forearm to the right.

"It works! It works, Eleanor!" Lifting the silver lid, Margo revealed what appeared to be three scrolls of paper tied with gold ribbons and laid together on the chest's velvet interior cushion. The cover script, they could just make out in the moonlight, was like that of the inlaid lettering on the lid of the larger chest.

"What could it be, Margo?"

"I don't know, but I know who might."

"Grandpas John and Joe!" Eleanor confirmed. "How can we get the scrolls into their hands? And how can we be sure the scrolls will do them any good?"

"We can't. But we can at least be ready should the scrolls be needed in court."

"How do you mean?"

"I mean we can sneak them into the courtroom and present them at the last, if all else fails."

"That sounds encouraging."

"Sorry, Eleanor; it's the best I can come up with. Besides, what else can we do?"

"Guess you're right."

"Come on, then, let's get home. I don't know about you, but I'm tired of these midnight outings."

"You said it, amiga!"

"We'll leave the chest where it is for the time being. Here, you take this scroll, and I'll keep the other two. Remember, not a word to anyone."

"Right!"

Thus resolved, the two detectives retraced their steps and soon were fast asleep in bed, the cares of life laid aside for another day.

The Court Rivals

The awaited day bloomed bright and fair in contrast to the past week of stormy weather. Yet the warm sun failed to dissipate the cloud of doubt that hovered in the minds of the spectators who packed the upper and lower sections of the courthouse. Amid the electric stir of movement and voices, none appeared to notice five visitors who sat in quiet meditation. Nor were any but Joe and Clay privy to the pronounced change come over Jack, who took in the court and all of life with new eyes. All remained veiled in mystery to the sea of humanity, and only those clued in to the last pieces of the puzzle could hope to guess at the trial's outcome. As the town clock struck one, the cloaked form of Judge Thornton appeared from a side door and advanced to the place he'd vacated eight weeks earlier after granting the stay.

"Court is now in session!" the judge announced with a *rap—rap* of his gavel. "It's my duty to remind those here present of the serious nature of these proceedings. Therefore I ask that order be maintained throughout the duration of the trial. You may proceed with the first witness, Mr. Martin."

"Thank you, your honor. If it pleases the court, I call on Mr. Jack Seaburn."

As the former bandit took the stand, Margo and Eleanor observed the pronounced change evident in his overall bearing and appearance. What happened to him?" Eleanor whispered, giving voice to the like thought of her friend.

"Yeah!" Margo whispered in return.

"Mr. Seaburn, as you know, two men stand accused of libel on the part of your former colleague. Point after point, he has challenged their testimony and suggested that he, himself, along with you and the deceased man, went after the gold in question on the bidding of these men. He further avows that he raised his pistols in self-defense, wishing only to protect himself, and that the firing of the one pistol was caused by a blow from behind. Here, as you'll recall, his testimony runs counter to that of the girls who insist on having been taken captive by Clay for ill use while he says he merely caught them in the act of spying. With these conflicting testimonies on record, it becomes all the more important that the court hear your own account of the episode."

The answer given in response to this appeal was matter-of-fact and direct. None present would have known or imagined it to be the same man who'd spoken briefly during the initial hearing. Had Clay not been aware of the trump cards held by Piper, he might have lost his composure; but he did know, and he'd been advised to hold fast his story regardless of Jack's testimony. So by the close of Jack's time in the witness stand, Clay was as self-assured as he'd been from the start. Meanwhile, a certain visitor seated with four other men looked long and hard at the pirate captain.

Having finished a brief cross-examination of Jack, Piper surprised the crowd by calling to the stand a secret witness by the name of Count Carazo.

"Do you, Count Carazo, swear to tell the truth, the whole truth, and nothing but the truth, so help you God?"

"I do." Again one of the visitors seated to the back on the lower level took in the face and name of the witness.

"I've asked you here today to bear witness to the legal ownership of a certain collection of gold coins. A general overview of the known history and facts surrounding the treasure has been presented in prior sessions. It would please the court if you'd explain your own background and how this relates to the issue of ownership and consequent issue of innocence or guilt on the part of those who stand trial here today."

"Your honor, counsel for the defense, ladies and gentlemen, I'm honored to give an account of the gold as requested; though how this may effect those on trial I can't assume to know. My name is Count Carazo, and my home city is that from which the coins were taken many years ago. I have on my person official papers spelling out legal ownership of what was once the fortune of a wealthy nobleman of my city. Upon his death, as the same documents show, he willed that the full measure of his estate and wealth in gold be turned over to the local government. A dispute arose, however, when the estate and treasure were claimed by a contentious man called Enrique Diaz. This man, acting in direct opposition to the government, had the gold portion of the estate shipped off in secret to an island in the Caribbean, where his son was known to live.

"A Spanish vessel, sent out straightway to retrieve the gold, found the island and its inhabitants under siege by pirates who were then pursued to American waters, where their galley was sunk and crew taken captive and turned over to the local authorities. Further visits to the island proved fruitless, and at length the treasure was given up for lost. I, being on official business in America and having heard news of the trial and discovered gold, was naturally curious. On inquiring into the matter, I met Mr. Piper and so was invited here today to give you the facts. The rest, ladies and gentlemen, I'm told you know."

"You'll note, your honor," Piper added, "the authenticity of the papers, including the official seal."

"Thank you, Mr. Piper. You may proceed."

"No further questions, your honor. I think the documents presented by the witness speak for themselves, and the truth of the testimony given. I yield the floor."

"Mr. Carazo," Martin began, "you attest to being familiar with ownership rights to the gold, even to the degree of carrying on your person legal documents pertaining to the same. Do you not think it odd, sir, to be bearing such papers on a business trip to America?"

"Objection, your honor! The relevance of the documents, not the Count's reason for carrying them, is of concern here."

"Objection overruled. Continue, Mr. Martin."

"Your honor! If you please, Mr. Carazo."

"If you insist. You see, my father was one of the officials who oversaw the case of the disputed will. It was he who kept the legal documents against the day in which news of the stolen wealth might bring resolution to the case. Many years elapsed, however, and no news came as my father had hoped. On his deathbed, he gave the documents into my hand, asking that I keep them as he had done. Naturally, when I was sent to America on business, I saw fit to take the documents along. For, as you know, I was mindful of the sunken pirate galley and so could not completely discount the chance of the gold being somewhere within the land to which I traveled."

"You say, Mr. Carazo, that a dispute existed between a certain nobleman and the government officials of your city. Can you tell the court why the person you mention disputed the same officials' claim to the estate?"

"Objection!"

"Sustained. Mr. Martin, I would ask that you keep to the facts of the case and evidence presented."

"Mr. Carazo, do you dispute all claims to the treasure other than that claim signified by the papers you possess?"

"It would seem logical, would it not?"

"This logic, then, thus excludes the nobleman and son you mentioned?" For the first time, a hint of agitation could be seen on the foreigner's face.

"But of course, what else?"

"Yet you will volunteer nothing more of the matter?"

"Really, I have nothing more to volunteer."

"Nothing?" The outburst, thundered from the back, caused all heads to turn in unison toward a prophetic-looking figure that stood and advanced toward the center aisle on his way to the witness stand.

"Order! Order in the court!" Judge Thornton cried, as a flurry of voices accompanied the bold challenger.

"Your honor, I beg your pardon for the disturbance," the stranger said when calm was restored. "But the testimony of the man before you is false and can be proven so, as he well knows."

"You will state your name and reason for objection."

"My name is Fernando Diaz. My father, Enrique Diaz, is none other than the nobleman spoken of by the witness."

"But this is extraordinary! And can you prove this claim to kinship?"

"I can, your honor," he replied, handing Martin the legal papers confirming his Christened name and place of birth, plus the letters of correspondence from his father concerning the estate, the legal will rendering the same to himself, and the corrupt local officials whose plotting forced him to send the gold portion by ship to the island of his son's residence. "Moreover, I can prove that the man seated in the witness stand is responsible, along with his father, for the injustice done to my family."

At this, the witness rose and declared, "I refuse to have such falsehood cast at myself or my father!"

Taking in the volatile nature of the conflict and wishing to avoid a spectacle, Judge Thornton hammered at his table in a decisive manner and stood to his feet, towering over the men and looking rather worn. "Given the turn of events, the court will recess for the space of one hour, during which time the present and volunteer witnesses will avail themselves of legal counsel prior to further testimony. Court is now recessed!"

The time allotted proved a Godsend to Martin and

a sobering wake-up call to Piper, who was not a man to give up without a fight. During the entire period, the men who accompanied Fernando into the court kept to their seats, unnoticed by the excited crowd. Margo and Eleanor also held fast to their places, feeling that deliverance had come at last in the reverent and powerful form of the man their grandpas had spoken of with love and respect: a man whose name struck a chord of memory in the mind of Margo's mom, who sat toward the front behind the witness area. When the court reconvened, Carazo took his place alongside of Piper whilst Fernando waited by the side of Martin. After rising and sitting with others at the re-entry of the judge, and then rising again to take a seat in the witness stand, Fernando looked out over the crowd of locals with a serene face. An older man, with well-kept white hair and beard and penetrating blue eyes, he captivated the audience with his almost saintly bearing, while giving Piper a growing sense of unease. Only Carazo and Clay viewed the intruder with disdain, perceiving their mutual need to contradict his testimony and turn the same against him.

"Mr. Diaz," Piper began, his body angled midway between the man addressed and the count. "On what grounds do you presume to accuse a respected guest of this court and emissary from Spain of slander? And may I remind you, sir, you are under oath!" The verbal jab met only with a settled gaze and look of doubt, as though the one scrutinized was seeking to discern the character of the man before him.

"It's no secret in Spain, your honor," said Fernando, choosing to address his reply not to Piper but to Judge Thornton, "how my father was plotted against by certain officials within the local government of our city. The names of these men are well-known to Mr. Carazo, as his own father planned and carried out the scheme to defame and rob my father of his honor, wealth, and legal right to the property and fortune of a benefactor who, being childless, named my father his sole inheritor."

"Ah, so you say, but where is your proof? Handwritten letters from your father? Come, sir!"

"The proof, your honor, was submitted to the proper authorities by the noted benefactor prior to his death, and afterward by my father himself when the matter came under dispute. As he would soon discover, however, the documents were destroyed by a certain officer in charge of review. Had my father's benefactor not made a duplicate set of wills, the case might have gone worse than it did. Though he suspected, still he submitted one of the remaining copies to the same Armando Carazo after being informed that the government held sway over the estate of the deceased. Grasping the nature of the case when this too failed, my father sent the final will copy along with a chest of gold to the island where I dwelt."

"Again, we have words but no proof! Surely, your honor, the witness would make a mockery of these proceedings. Are we to accept your word over that of an official dignitary sent from the government of which you speak ill?"

"Your honor, it's not my intention or desire to speak ill of my country or people. And I think it will go easier on the man of whom the counsel refers if he would choose to admit the truth. Nevertheless, let it be known to all who hear me this day that my father was cleared many years ago of the false charged made by Armando Carazo and his fellow conspirators. Also, while Carazo doubted my father's testimony concerning the final copy of the will, he was unable to refute his word until the document should be searched out; to this end he used his position to secure a Spanish ship, the captain being a business associate who was easily got for a price. Yet the document was never discovered by the captain who arrived at the island only to find the Spanish war ship just returned from its battle with the pirates."

"And the document? Can it be, ladies and gentlemen, that this witness is to be believed on his testimony alone? Show us the proof, sir, for the weight of your accusations demands it!" For a moment Fernando appeared to hesitate, adding wind to the flame of doubt ignited by Piper's terse ultimatum.

"It is my belief, your honor," he said at last, "that

a further airing of either Joseph Whitaker's or John Stanley's testimony will bring the satisfaction of proof requested."

"Ah, you see gentlemen of the jury, there is no proof! Why, your honor, should a request of this nature be considered?"

"It is a peculiar request, it would seem; yet little about the case before us has been usual. Would you agree, Mr. Piper? Therefore I see no harm in further testimony from either Mr. Whitaker of Mr. Stanley."

"Your honor, I yield the floor."

"No further questions, your honor." Martin's words, marveled at by the crowd of onlookers who gawked as the surprise witness returned to his seat, were followed by his requesting Mr. Joseph Whitaker to take the stand. Joe, tired from his stay in prison, yet encouraged by the wondrous appearance of Fernando, wandered over the sea of familiar faces with his eyes before focusing in on the intent countenance of Martin.

"Mr. Whitaker, you've heard the testimony of Mr. Fernando Diaz. Can you elaborate on the matter at hand? Are you aware, as he affirms, of a certain will pertaining to the treasure and estate of the benefactor he mentioned?" Had anyone in the room been privy to the inner thoughts of Martin, they may well have wondered at the power of conviction with which he made his inquiry. He was, in reality, filled with doubt. Only the force of Fernando's presence, coupled with the certainty of his bold assertions, gave him the courage to speak in a way befitting confidence of victory, though this was by no means definite in his mind.

"Fernando did give John and me a second chest containing documents he affirmed to be of great value. But we weren't given to know the nature of the documents at the time of our departure from the island; rather he asked that we keep the chest in a safe place until such time as he might inquire after it or give instructions for its use. Of course, we did as requested under oath. Now that Fernando's directed, however, either John or I will be glad to retrieve the chest from its hiding place."

"Objection! Can it be possible, your honor, that these delaying tactics be permitted in this court?"

"Objection sustained. Ample time has been allowed each of the attorneys. The final verdict to be rendered today must, therefore, be based on evidence given to date. You may continue, Mr. Martin." Instead the shrill tone of Margo's pleading voice rang throughout the chamber, causing the judge to sit back in amazement.

"Wait! You must believe Grandpa Joe! Here!" Pulling at her bag and Eleanor's sleeve at the same time, she lifted into the air the sealed scrolls that had been stowed away in silent anticipation of this moment. Before the judge recovered himself, Margo made her way to the man she felt needed the documents.

"Mr. Martin, if you please!" the visibly agitated judge let out. Martin, encouraged by the development, took the scrolls from Margo and conveyed the same into his hands. Noting the familiar seal on one of the documents, Judge Thornton peered down at the bold little personage before him and asked, "Young lady, where did you get these papers?"

"In the cave, sir!" The reply brought a ripple of laughter from the relieved crowd of locals.

"I see. And I suppose this cave is the same hiding place mentioned by you, Mr. Whitaker?"

"It is, your honor; though how my granddaughter found the chest I can't say."

"Your honor," Piper interrupted, "the documents are sealed. And, as you know, they could be forged or even irrelevant to the case."

"Thank you, Mr. Piper; I'm aware of these facts. If you don't mind." At that, Piper returned to his seat. "Young lady, you may also be seated. Mr. Whitaker, do you not think it odd to have kept such documents sealed up in a cave all these years? Did it never occur to you that the papers in your possession could be of importance—even of relevance to these proceedings?"

"That it did, your honor, to both John and me. Yet it wasn't right, we figured, to break our oath to Fernando. He'd been true as ever a friend could be to us, and we owed him our lives besides. So you see we thought only of honoring his request."

"Indeed. Mr. Martin, do you have any further questions?"

"None, your honor."

"Mr. Piper?"

"Your honor, in view of the evidence presented, I wish to call upon Count Carazo, that he may speak in his own defense."

Weighing the matter before him, Judge Thornton announced: "This court will recess for the space of fifteen minutes, after which time each counsel will be given opportunity for a final calling forth of witnesses. The jury will then retire to consider its verdict." As he pounded the table with his well-worn gavel, Margo turned to her friend, feeling a shared sense of release and confidence in hope of their grandfathers' ultimate triumph. Clay, failing to miss a single detail of the exchanges past, found means to confer with Piper on a matter of apparent urgency. Fernando, having rejoined his brothers and Captain Clark, sat in private consultation over the anticipated testimony to come. Maria, wondering at her daughter's combination of ingenuity and mischief, prayed to God for a swift and happy end to the trial. As in answer to her prayers, the judge reappeared and court action resumed.

"Your honor," Piper announced when all were seated, "I'm pleased to inform the court of Count Carazo's desire that another take his place as the final witness. He wishes the court to know that there's nothing to add to his testimony. And that being a Spanish official, he reserves the right to refer any verdict of this court to the authorities of Spain under whose noble auspices he serves and to whom he owes obedience."

"The court recognizes Mr. Carazo's privilege as a subject of Spain."

"Thank you, your honor. I now call upon Captain Bart Clay." A ruffle of whispers subdued by the rap of the gavel accompanied Clay to the witness stand. Why the defense counsel chose to employ the pirate's former title none could but wonder at. "Captain Clay, can you tell the jury what occurred prior to the chase that ended with the sinking of your ship?"

"Well sir, it ain't that I'm proud to confess it, but that horde of gold this fellow from Spain and the others keep going on about, why, it's nowhere but at the bottom of the sea off these here parts." A second flurry of whispers erupted from the incredulous crowd.

"Can you prove this assertion?"

"Aye, by my life I can, and many a long year cooped up in that foul prison. Mark my words, it's as I say. Wasn't it my ship that dropped anchor off that island? Do you think me a fool? Do you think we'd a left the gold and other booty? No sir! And we 'bout got away with it, 'cept for them Spaniards. We gave 'em a fight, to a man we did! But they took us with them big guns, and that's all of it. There lies your secret: buried with my ship for all time on the ocean floor, see. As for the loot in the cave, it's pirate spoils, as ever was. And them two liars that done set up me, Jack and Butch, why they're no better than I was before prison. No sir, it ain't right! And I want justice!" To the shock and dismay of Joe and John, Clay's words had a clear and moving effect on the unsuspecting jury. He'd played the part with flawless ease of deception come of long practice, and none of the jury members saw through the veneer of outward earnest to the base inner reality. Even Martin was stymied by the wild card played by his rival attorney, as his futile attempt at cross-examination showed.

"Mr. Martin, your final witness!" Judge Thornton's directive was answered, much to Martin's amazement, by the sudden movement of a giant of a man to the front of the courtroom. Like Fernando, the man had a white beard and well-kept appearance, yet he was older and gave the impression of one who'd come with his own concern in mind. Arriving at Martin's side, the man gave him a look of assurance, thus prompting the baffled attorney to trust in providence.

"After a few words in private with the volunteer witness, Martin announced, "Your honor, I call brother Rodolfo to the stand." The judge, assuming the action to have been planned, took in the striking features of the witness. Clay also studied the man who took the seat he'd just vacated. Something about the face troubled him. Try as he might, however, he failed to place it.

"Brother Rodolfo," Martin began with some hesitation, "you've come to volunteer testimony pertaining to the case. The floor is yours, sir." To the side, Piper listened with growing amusement, noting the straining after straws his bettered associate had been forced to at the last.

"Your honor, members of the jury, it's with a sad heart I come before you today. No, it cannot be that deceit will prevail over truth. Nor can it be that two innocent men should endure a punishment that belongs to another: a man as cruel and bloody as any cutthroat that ever roamed the seas. If he doubts my words, let him be reminded who I am and of the savagery unleashed upon a community of monks living in peace and missionary service amid a tropical island in the Caribbean. To this island, the man of whom I speak came with his brigands, seeking gold that perishes with use and leaving bloodied corpses in his path. He remembers, no doubt, the four men he had tortured to death in hopes of finding out the gold." A grimace came upon Clay as the witness spoke, his words cutting like a sword of judgment. "I was their leader, the one charged with their care, even as we all cared for the sick and needy of the islands. Did he care for our men, our work, our faith? No, your honor, no more than he cares for the one he now seeks to destroy.

"Had he succeeded, he'd have taken my own life as well. I see, he does remember." Clay glared at his rival, feeling the swell of emotion in the hushed crowd that had the unusual effect of preventing a word of objection from Piper. "But why, I wonder, did he choose a cross as an ultimate form of torture? There he left me to either confess to the gold's location or die a lingering death beneath the tropical sun. The scars remain, as he may imagine, here on this body tortured at his will and here on this heart that witnessed the deaths of those slain at his command. Will such a man be set free by this assembly to inflict more damage on society? I shudder to think! No! He will surely account for his deeds. Further as the judge of these proceedings knows, the documents presented earlier are legal and authentic, bearing additional testimony to the truth of brother Fernando's words. Am I correct in so saying, your honor?"

"You are correct," Judge Thornton acknowledged, nodding gravely.

"The content of said document being the will of Enrique Diaz's benefactor, the will of Enrique Diaz conveying the same estate and wealth to his son Fernando, and the will of Fernando Diaz granting the treasure involved to a certain Maria Whitaker by the hand of Joseph Whitaker in due time and at Fernando's bidding?"

"That is also correct," the judge added to the astonishment of his hearers.

"As to the tale of sunken treasure, let it be recorded that two witnesses present here today can testify that no such gold as that mentioned by the previous witness was taken from the island on the pirate ship's departure. For the real treasure was hidden with the remainder of our brethren in a place unknown and undiscovered by Clay and his men." At this, Clay's countenance darkened, his clenched fists betraying his sudden and apparent feeling of regret over the missed opportunity. "There, ladies and gentlemen, sits the man whose life of unrepentant banditry has led to the ruination of all too many lives; the evidence of his crimes can also be attested to by the captain whose ship brought my brothers and me to this shore. And I see our coming was not in vain, but that justice will prevail in the end. If there's anything to forgive, God knows I hold no ill will toward any man. However I cannot see my good friend Fernando, or Mr. Whitaker and Mr. Stanley, brought low by a man who cares nothing for his fellow creatures, including the one he killed by accident two months ago, as I'm to understand. Surely, it is enough!"

As with Martin's failed efforts in cross-examining of Clay, Piper failed to gain any advantage over the witness seated before him. And in short order, the visitor stood and exited at Judge Thornton's bidding, who then inquired, "Is the captain spoken of by brother Rodolfo here present?"

"I am, your honor!" The voice came from a tall man who arose to the right of the seated monastic brethren.

"Will you testify under oath to aspects of the report

given by the witness concerning Captain Clay and his men?"

"I will, sir!" he replied, leaving his place and walking amid the excited gaze of the spectators.

"And the witness to the murders of the four monastic members, will he come forth to testify under oath to the truth or falsity of the accusations made?"

Rising from Fernando's side, the third brother replied, "I will!" The middle-aged monk called Brother Andrew reflected on the train of events that began with Clay's incursion. He'd been the first to reach Rodolfo in his extremity, the detailed account of which he rendered in full to the court. Piper, unable to counter the weight of evidence presented, including the chilling account of Captain Clark, watched with others as a spirit of malevolent defiance took hold of Clay in subdued looks of rage that confirmed, along with testimony given, the unanimous decision of the jury.

After a brief recess, the verdict came forth. "Your honor, we the members of the jury find the defendant called Clay to be guilty concerning the charge of abduction. We find the same defendant and Mr. Seaburn to be not guilty of theft, given the peculiar nature of the case. Furthermore, we find John Stanley and Joseph Whitaker to be not guilty on any count, including libel." It was over, Margo and Eleanor realized with relief, a sense of joy filling their hearts even as Judge Thornton leaned forward to render his final opinion.

"As you know, serious accusations have been made here today that go beyond the primary focus of this trial and jurisdiction of this court. On careful examination of documents received and testimony given, it is the view of this court that Captain Clay be held without bond until such time as a naval court should review his case and pronounce judgment. The witness who goes by the name of Count Carazo will be deported forthwith to Spain, there to give account of his misleading testimony and use of spurious documents within this place. The gold portion of the Diaz family estate will be managed in accordance with the legal documents submitted by Margo Whitaker on behalf of Joseph Whitaker and his daughter Maria: the rightful claimant to the fortune. As to any supposed conflict, there can be no need of concern on the part of Mr. Diaz or those he wishes to benefit over legal action from Spanish officials, for it's all too evident that such officials have no proper legal claim to the estate. Court is now dismissed!"

The Treasure

"Grandpa Joe! Grandpa Joe!" Margo cried, approaching the front yard with Eleanor at her side. "We solved the mystery!"

A week had come and gone since the trial's end, during which time Fernando and his brothers stayed on as special guests at the Whitaker's home for three days prior to departing with Captain Clark and his crew. Within those golden days and hours, Fernando told story after story of his life at sea and on the island. As to the disputed estate and treasure, the matter was resolved in his home city a number of years back. In spite of the evidence, Carazo had determined to claim what his father had failed to gain by craft and deceit. Nor would the self-proclaimed count rest, even after two unsuccessful trips to the island, until the honor of his family name was restored.

The recent trip to America and the site of the pirates' defeat had been a last ditch effort on Carazo's part to uncover clues to the treasure. Yet no leads were to be found, Joe and John having kept their oath of secrecy. Not until news of the trial reached his hearing did Carazo seek a means of influence in order to gain his objective; this means came in the person of Piper, who was soon drawn into the count's scheme unawares. Meanwhile, back in Spain, the once disputed estate served at Fernando's bidding as an institute for orphaned children: a home branch of the Monastery of Santa Maria; this too was known to Carazo and had been for some time.

With these details and other evidence in mind, Margo and Eleanor strode across the Whitaker's porch on the heels of Margo's declaration and sat down alongside their grandparents.

"Mystery? What mystery would that be?" Grandpa Joe asked.

"The mystery of Santa Maria!" Eleanor replied with equal pride of accomplishment.

"Ah, of course, Santa Maria! We knew you two would get it sooner or later," said John.

"But grandpa, is it true?"

"True? Well now, let's first hear what you have to say."

"We think there's more to the benefactor of Mr. Enrique Diaz than even Fernando is willing to reveal," Eleanor began.

"Is that a fact?" Joe remarked.

"Yes, Grandpa! You see, the way we figure, Mr. Diaz must have been related to his benefactor in some way. Why else would he be named as sole heir at his age?"

"There's more too!" Eleanor insisted, picking up the train of logic the girls had pursued in putting the pieces of the puzzle together.

"Indeed!" said her grandpa.

"Much more, we suspect," she continued. "For the sharp and bitter rivalry between the Diaz and Carazo families hints at something beyond local government corruption."

"You mean Armando Carazo, I presume?" Joe asked.

"At first," said Margo, "and then his son later on. We're not positive about the connection, yet we think it likely that Enrique Diaz had an elder brother, and that this same brother married a member of the Carazo family, and by some means acquired a large fortune. Then tragedy struck, perhaps involving the death of a child, as this would account for friction in the marriage and between the families. The wife's death, some time later, could have been a further blow to family relations. Then with the elder brother's demise, the issue of the inheritance might have become a main point of contention. Having lost his wife and child, it makes sense that this brother would make out a secret will and entrust the same to Enrique to be used for the good of their family."

"Getting wind of the will," Eleanor concluded, "Mr. Carazo seized the opportunity offered by his position within the local government and pursued the course of action described by Fernando. As we know, the Diaz brothers were prepared for this treachery and so were able to frustrate Carazo's scheme, and in time, by Enrique's order after his brother's death, ship the gold portion of wealth to Fernando in the Caribbean."

"And the rest we know," Margo observed, looking at her grandpa with a mixture of pride and doubt. "Or do we?"

"And did we get the missing pieces right?" Eleanor asked.

"My land, if they ain't a pair!" said John.

"You mostly did!" Joe pronounced. "Only Enrique's brother inherited a fortune when the father came to a mysterious end at sea. The *Treasure of Santa Maria* they called it, as the gold was found in the catacombs of an ancient monastic order long since abandoned and come to ruin. The boys were young at the time of their father's death. And the elder brother learned all too late about the Carazo family, whose daughter was encouraged to marry him as a means to his wealth. For years, she squandered his riches and lived as she pleased. Then she contracted a fatal illness, leaving him a careworn man with no children, for the one and only child born early on in the marriage failed to reach his twelfth year."

"Grandpa John, there's one matter that puzzles us."

"What's that, darling?"

"It's about the sea caves."

"Sea caves! What about 'em?"

"Well, to be honest, we were wondering why you and Grandpa Joe decided to hide the treasure there instead of somewhere else."

"Yeah," Margo asked, "why did you?"

"If that don't beat all! What do you say, Joe?"

"I 'spect, you'd best give the girls an answer."

"Fair enough! Did you two happen to notice anything unusual about that mountain retreat?"

The girls thought for a moment. Then Margo ventured, "Now that you mention it, we knew you and Grandpa Joe used the cave over the years, though you kept it a secret, yet it's clear only a small person no bigger than Eleanor or me could make it through the main entryway."

"Right!" Eleanor lightened. "And the sun!"

"Yes, the sun marked a path across the interior of the cave leading to my discovery of the key last summer."

"And did you search out the entry of the sun?" Joe probed.

"We tried, but the face of the hillside leading up to the light's point of entry was too steep to climb, so we let it go." Margo's reply brought nods of concurrence from the two elders. "Nonetheless we wondered about it, as we did the great stone that sealed off all but a slender place of access into the cave."

"Did you happen to notice where the sun hit in mid-summer?" Joe pursued.

Reflecting, Margo sat upright and announced, "The wall! The wall behind the stone table on which the silver chest and its Bible rested! Of course! Why didn't I see it?"

"You did see it, you just didn't comprehend what you saw. Now do you know the answer?"

"Sure, Grandpa! The treasure chest was hidden in the wall behind the Bible; it must have been. Still I don't understand."

"I think you do," Grandpa John concluded. "The Bible is the true and lasting treasure. Through our knowledge of God we have the wisdom to use the wealth of this world without becoming its slave or victim."

"Like Clay and Butch?" asked Eleanor.

Her grandpa nodded. "Like Clay and Butch!"

"Then it was there all the time, right under our noses!"

"I'm afraid so, my dear," said Joe.

"But Grandpa, when did the treasure get moved to the sea caves? How'd you do it? And why could Eleanor and I not see the outline of its hiding place in the wall, as we did with the second chest?"

"To tell you the truth, we were surprised you discovered the hiding place you mention, for we'd taken great care in the work of hiding the crevice lines. At any rate, we're glad you did find the chest, you may be sure."

"And had you discovered the third chest, you'd have found the real store of gold!" said John.

"Real store? What do you mean, Grandpa?"

"What I mean is it's there, right in that very cave where we left it, sure as I'm sitting here!"

"Then ... then ... what was it the pirates found in the sea caves that night?" Margo asked.

"Fool's gold, that's what, collected over years of surveying one antiquity shop after another in search of the elusive treasure map," John admitted.

"You mean, they made counterfeit coins out of fool's gold?"

"Iron and copper pyrites!" her grandpa stated. "And we were just crazy enough to keep a collection of the coins."

"Little could we have known, at the time, what use they'd serve us later," John added.

"Grandpa, what if the pirates had caught on?"

"We considered the possibility. However the caves are plenty dark, even with the aid of a torch. And we guessed the men would be in haste to depart from our coast, as it would be easy for us to have the authorities after them. Had they thought to test the metal, we planned to profess ignorance and so hope for their departure in either case. As it turned out, you and Eleanor changed the course of everyone's plans, and, it seems, that's the way it was meant to be."

The girls paused in reflection. Then Margo inquired, "Grandpa Joe, do you suppose God knew all along what would happen in the end? I mean, do you think it's all somehow part of God's plan for our lives?"

"I tell you, I don't reckon it matters what we think of such things. What matters is doing what we know to be right to the best of our ability. God knows what sort of mischief people can get into, that's sure, but God doesn't plan it; that's man's doing. And the wise person learns to keep well out of harm's way. Ain't that so, John!"

"Sure as you can count on trials in this life. And we're real proud of the way you two handled the trouble of them scoundrels, including Jack before his change."

"Aw, it wasn't much," Eleanor sported.

"Much? I dare say, it's a sight more than most kids your age go through," Joe returned with a twinkle.

"Perhaps, then, these young heroes won't mind helping with dinner?" Glancing round at the open screen door, Margo beheld the radiant face of her mother.

"Maria, we were just talking about you!" Joe submitted.

"You were, eh? I see! How about it, young lady?"

"But mom, we were only getting started. Besides, Grandpa's right! We were talking about you, about the treasure of Santa Maria!"

"Why, I couldn't have put it better myself," said Joe. "And, wouldn't you know, it'd come from your own daughter's mouth."

"I'm not surprised; it seems everyone's interested in treasure these days. What's a body to do?'

"That's just the point!" John replied, picking up on Joe's comment. "It's what we've been telling the girls all along. The real treasure is here in the home and family."

"Like the Monastery of Santa Maria!" said Eleanor.

"Right you are!" her grandpa seconded.

"And the monastery was named after the old abandoned one in Spain. Isn't that so, Mom?"

"It's likely, dear. But that's another life and far away."

"Not so far as may seem, given recent events," Joe observed.

"Perhaps you're right. All the same, we could do with a bit less excitement around here for awhile, don't you agree?" A chorus of laughter met this comment, ending with the departure of Eleanor and Margo.

Soon the seasons turned over, bringing in the regenerative feeling of springtime. News had come from Captain Clark of the successful voyage to and from the Caribbean island. A joyous celebration had highlighted the brothers' return. The captain and crew were welcomed as guests. And the trip back to America, after a two-day stay and further trade stops, was happily graced with favorable winds. Meanwhile, gossip abounded in Witherspoon over the gold, though talk of the trial soon faded after its completion. Why Joe decided to keep the treasure chest on hand none could guess, nor had anyone persuaded either him or John to speak of the matter. It was Joe's decision, and that was that! Also it was made clear by Judge Thornton that Joe had complete oversight of the gold's safekeeping until such time as Maria should determine its use.

Still, none but Joe, John, Margo, and Eleanor knew the truth about the real gold and its location, the fool's gold being shut up in the Whitaker's attic. Not till the end of school and beginning of summer did the porch talk turn to the anticipated trip to Lookout Mountain. Margo's father, a fisherman by trade and so often gone to sea for days on end, had been persuaded by Joe to revisit the new campsite with the whole family come berry-picking time. Eleanor's parents had also decided to go along in the wake of her pleading and John's encouragement. So plans were set.

It was a happy, peaceful season for the close-knit community of Witherspoon. Picnics in the park, visits to the swimming hole, kite-flying ventures, sailboat rides and sandcastle displays: all this and more filled the off-school days with a sense of collective pleasure. None could guess, not even the girls' parents, the real reason behind their desire to visit the mountain sanctuary. Nor did the two couples notice the extra gear packed by either grandparent. It was a secret, and the girls promised their grandpas to keep it so.

When the day of departure arrived, Maria and her husband gave in to Grandpa Joe's insistence on leaving the chest of gold behind in the attic. Ask as they had for days to have it moved for safekeeping in the bank, he refused to budge. And there was no getting around it; his mind was made up and the legal right remained his in this regard according to Fernando's will. Hence, after locking the house up tight, the Whitakers loaded up the wagon and headed out in the direction of the desired campground, with Eleanor and her family some hundred-yards to the rear in their rig. On reaching camp, the men and boys wasted no time in setting up the tents while the girls aided their mothers with other preparations anxious to visit the mountain grotto.

Come morning, the girls weren't surprised to see their two brothers run off after breakfast to look for crawdads in the nearby stream, leaving them to hike up to the cave with their grandparents. The other men had gone off ahead of the boys early on, knowing their sons would follow the trail up river. Maria and Isabel, glad for time to themselves, declined the girls' invitation to visit the cave.

"There it is!" the girls shouted on rounding the final bend leading up to the cave's entry. Running ahead, they peered into the opening and then looked back to signal the way to the sacred place. The thrill of the moment was quick to wear off, however, as they once again realized the impossibility of anyone larger than themselves gaining access to the cave. The fact had by no means slipped the minds of the elders, nor had they felt it worthy of mention along the way.

"Grandpa John, the entry, we forgot, it's too small for a big person to get through."

"Not to worry, Eleanor! God put that boulder in our way for a reason. Or didn't we tell you?"

"Tell us what, Grandpa?"

"The tale of the rock's rolling down the mountain not seven years past."

"That's certain! For me and John were here seven years ago, and that rock was sitting firm as ever up yonder on the hillside overlooking the cave's mouth."

"It would seem," said John, "there's nothing but for you two to carry out the final steps of Fernando's will."

"You mean," asked Margo, looking with doubt at her elders, "we're to bring out the treasure on our own?"

"Can't see any way round it. Can you?" added Joe.

The girls looked at each other, over at the great stone, and back at their grandparents. "I suppose not," said Eleanor, puzzling over the prospect.

"But Grandpa, why did we leave the fool's gold locked up in the attic, as though it were the real gold?"

"The answer is simple, Margo, if you think it over. After all, don't you suppose the local chatter about the gold, plus word of the trial, might have reached the ears of men acquainted with the likes of Clay?"

"I guess so."

"And don't you think me and John would have been on the alert for signs of danger these past months, especially given the punishment meted out to Clay by the naval court?"

The girls nodded.

"Then you'll not be shaken by news of bandits here in our parts: former members of Clay's crew come to pirate away the treasure he failed to loot."

"Why didn't you tell us?"

"We, ourselves, didn't learn of the pirates' scheme till a fortnight ago, Eleanor," Joe acknowledged. "Nor were we aware Clay's men had been released from prison. It's a good thing we did get wind of their plans, as we'll explain later, for we'd about concluded that no real danger was to come on the heels of Clay's execution after all."

"But they're sure to be taken in the trap you've set, right Joe!"

"Let's hope so, John. For the present, however, there's a store of gold to withdraw from this mountain.

And we're counting on you scouts to make good the deed."

"We're game, Grandpa! But how can we know the bandits will be caught?"

"I admit, we can't. All the same, we made sure word got out to the sheriff concerning the treasure chest's location, and deputies will be keeping watch each night of our absence. If or when a break-in occurs, they've been instructed to take pirates and fool's gold into custody. There's an end of it! Now what do you say we get that gold!"

"Sure, Grandpa!" said Margo, motioning to Eleanor. In little time, the two were at the appropriate wall, the light flooding its surface as expected. To their relief, they found the cover stone to be relatively easy to maneuver in comparison to the stone that concealed the hidden scroll chest. In less than an hour, with the aid of their grandpas' tools, the girls worked the second stone from its place.

"Here, you take one end and I'll take the other," Eleanor suggested, pulling the heavy chest from its solitary place with the help of her friend. It was all they could do to move the box out into the open air in view of the elders. On completing this feat, the two sat down with their backs against the massive stone and looked with satisfaction on the finished task. Just then, they noticed the reflective silence of the men who they thought would be overjoyed at the sight of the treasure. What could it mean? A flood of images from their grandpas' stories came to mind in the train of this unspoken question and brought the granddaughters into sudden sympathy with their elders.

"That's fine, girls, just fine!" said John, breaking the mood of melancholy.

"To think," Joe noted, "all the effort we spent in searching out this treasure, and now we can't wait to be rid of it!" The two men laughed, causing the girls to join in the odd merriment.

"It's blood-money, no doubt!" And I shudder to think how many a poor wretch has suffered on its account, not to mention our own ill-fated voyage."

"Well, it's over now," Joe announced, looking at the girls with pride. "And we trust the good this gold will do may serve to erase its tainted history. What do you say?"

Margo gazed at her grandpa with sympathy of understanding that belied her youth and relative lack of experience. "It's a good thing the gold is going to help people in need!"

"I think so too!" said Eleanor. "One thing's certain: it sure is heavy!" The men laughed as the girls felt the pride of a job well done.

"Shall we go?" John suggested, feeling a sudden itch to be off fishing.

"Grandpa, if you don't mind, we'd like to stay behind in the cave."

"Please, Grandpa!" Margo appealed. The men looked with pleasant surprise at the granddaughters who'd come, as they had years ago, to discover the real treasure of the mountain. For one seeking retreat, the cave and its inner sanctuary space was the near-unto-perfect place.

"We understand. Go along, then; only see you're back at camp in time for lunch. And pray they catch those pirates while you're at it."

"We will, Grandpa! We will!" Eleanor promised, her words carried off by the breeze as she and Margo disappeared behind the massive stone.

"That's that!" Joe remarked. "Come on, let's get this chest off to camp and grab our poles!"

"You're on!"

Once again, the girls experienced a special peace in the cave's tranquil setting. As they sat on stone benches looking up at the treetops and blue sky beyond, they soon found themselves caught-up in the peculiar atmosphere of the cavern. An hour passed in this state, their words and thoughts centered on all they'd been through since the past summer. Another hour passed, hunger alone driving the two out into the open air on route to camp and lunch.

"Oh mother, you should see the cavern; it's so lovely in there, and so peaceful," Margo exclaimed.

"It's just a simple cave with a sweet sense of God's presence. We can't explain it."

"We believe you, children, but it's past lunch-time,"

Isabel observed. "The men and boys have already finished and gone off to fish and swim.

"Then, where's the treasure?"

"Treasure?" Maria questioned.

The girls glanced at one another warily. "Oh nothing, just a fancy," Margo evaded. It was clear their grandfathers were taking no chances. The threat of which they'd spoken must be real indeed, else why the evident caution? And where, they wondered, had the chest been hidden? Yet it didn't seem to matter. They were all together. And the two friends would enjoy four more days of high adventure on the mountain, including ample time in their favorite wilderness spot.

As it happened, Grandpas Joe and John had waited for the right opportunity and then placed the treasure chest out of sight under cover of the Whitaker wagon. There it remained, untouched and unexamined throughout the family vacation. Only when news of the attempted burglary and consequent arrest of the bandits was received by the families on their return to Witherspoon did the full truth come out.

"But why, Father? Why all the secrecy? Would it not have been better to let us know all this months ago?"

"We'd thought of that, Maria, but the risk was too great."

"It's so," John stressed, "for the rogues would have stopped at nothing to get their hands on the gold."

"And to revenge Clay's death," Joe pointed out.

"Revenge?" asked Maria. "How could they get revenge?"

"Right," her husband insisted, "especially if the gold were placed in a bank vault where it belongs."

"We considered that too," said Joe. "Then a month or so after the trial of Clay we received this note." Pulling a folded piece of paper from his pocket, he read the words marked out on its surface as the two families stood about the wagons.

> *You done him in, sure as we know. Now it's your turn to pay. And pay you shall, for every inch of rope that brung Clay low. Watch for it! Mind, by summer's end: give up the gold, or give up your lives. The Bull's Eye Tavern, that's the place. Have an answer by week's end. You know our play. Just think on giving the gold up to the bank, and we'll have them kids! Any word from your mouth, and you'll feel the edge! See to it, or else!*

"But the trial and execution of Clay occurred over a month ago." Maria's observation brought a further nod of recognition from Joe.

"Meaning the pirate note must have arrived not long before our trip to Lookout Mountain," Margo interjected.

"Not two weeks, in fact," John recalled.

"So, you see, we had no choice but to leave the bait and notify the sheriff as to our anticipated visitors."

"That would explain the secrecy," Isabel allowed.

"Couldn't be helped, I'm afraid." John's assertion was met with looks of sympathy on the part of Margo's and Eleanor's parents.

"Well then, that's an end to the whole business!" Joe announced, the signs of relief visible on his tawny face.

"Let's hope so," Maria commented, chagrined by the news of pirates in her domain.

"Grandpa, Grandpa, the treasure!"

"Ah yes, I almost forgot." Motioning to John, the two men lifted the chest from its place in the wagon and set it to the side of the road. "Margo, would you run and tell Sheriff Nick it's time to move the real gold to the bank?"

"Can I go too?" Eleanor pleaded.

"You might as well, dear," Isabel granted. "You can help us unload when you return."

Anxious to assist their grandpas, the liberated pair took to their heels, glad for the happy conclusion to a long adventure. Or was it over? Had they reached the end of the path Margo came upon that day in the mountain a year ago? Time alone would tell. Besides, they'd found the real treasure, after all, or perhaps they'd discovered anew what had been theirs from the start: family and friends, neighbors, community, and the many simple gifts and blessings often missed or taken for granted in life.

As they rounded the bend on course to the sheriff's office, a strong desire took hold of them both. Before long they were running in carefree abandonment toward the cliff and lighthouse overlooking the bay and broad ocean beyond. The setting sun filled the sky with a bright golden hue that blended in the warm breeze flowing like water over the girls' skin.

"Do you ever wonder what it's like on the island?" Eleanor mused. Margo had wondered. She'd often dreamed of hoisting sail on route to the tropical community, a place she felt she'd come to know through stories and the meeting of Fernando and his fellow monks.

"Sure, I do."

"About the people, the birds, the plants, and fish and just everything?"

"Sure, everything. And I wonder about the estate used as a center for orphans and other needs there in Spain. Wouldn't it be fun to visit both places someday, even to help out?"

"It would be!" said Eleanor.

Rapt in the reverie, the two sat together and gazed beyond the distant horizon, savoring the peace of home and dreams of future adventures.

"Bonita Santa Maria!" said Margo, crowning the moment.

"Bonita Santa Maria!" Eleanor replied, rising with her friend.

Character List

Margo, an adventurous eleven-year old tomboy

Grandpa Joe, a retired sailor and Margo's grandfather

Maria, Joe's daughter and Margo's mom

Eleanor, Margo's best friend

Grandpa John, Eleanor's grandfather and Joe's old sea-mate

Isabel, John's daughter and Eleanor's mom

Old Rupert, a retired sailor

Fernando Diaz, a wild youth who leaves Spain for the Caribbean

Enrique Diaz, Fernando's father and son of Manuel

Manuel Diaz, first to find of the

Treasure of Santa Maria

Carlos Carazo, fellow treasure hunter who betrays and murders Manuel

Armando Carazo, archrival of the Diaz family

Count Carazo, Armando's son and Fernando's main rival

Captain Clay, a notorious pirate

Jack Seaburn, pirate and Clay's fellow convict

Butch, Mediterranean pirate of the African treasure hunt

Judge Thornton, presiding trial judge

Martin, the prosecuting attorney

Piper, the defense attorney

Captain Clark, a friend of Old Rupert's

Rodolfo, a giant monk who once sailed with Captain Clay

Witherspoon townsfolk

People in Spain

African tribal members

Fernando's crew

Monastic members

Caribbean pirates

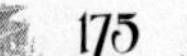

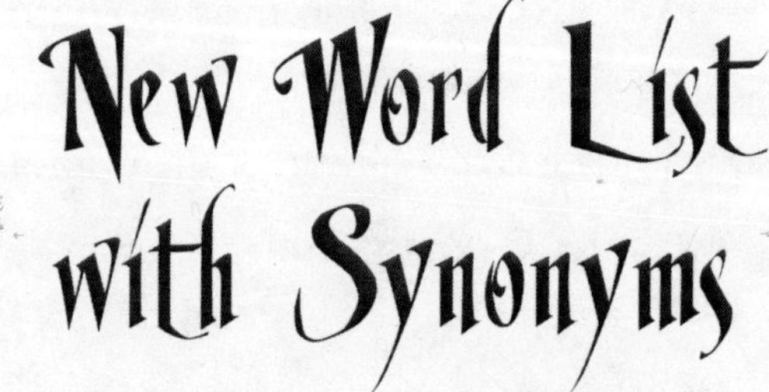

New Word List with Synonyms

FOR YOUNG READERS

ague (n.): acute fever, chill
aloof (adj.): cool, reserved
alluring (v.): attractive, tempting
amassed (v.): collected, gathered
anguish (n.): distress, grief
anomaly (n.): oddity, rarity
anticipated (v.): expected, prepared for
apparition (n.): manifestation, presence
apprised (v.): made aware, informed
austere (n.): severe, difficult
avowed (v.): declared, sworn

berth (n.): place, spot
calamity (n.): disaster, hardship
camaraderie (n.): comradeship, friendship
chagrined (n.): dismayed, distressed
coerced (v.): forced, pressured
confidant (n.): friend, crony
culminating (v.): concluding, ending
dilemma (n.): impasse, problem
disdain (v.): contempt, scorn
dismay (v.): alarm, distress
dissipate (v.): dispel, disperse
dissuade (v.): discourage, urge not to
diversion (n.): distraction, amusement
divulge (v.): reveal, make known
elapsed (v.): went by, passed
eliciting (v.): causing, bringing forth
emphatic (adj.): assertive, insistent
encompass (n.): cover, involve
ensued (v.): followed, resulted
exuberance (n.): enthusiasm, liveliness
exuded (v.): expressed, showed
flanked (adj.): edged, fringed
flustered (v.): ruffled, shaken
forgo ((v.): do without, skip
garb (n.): clothing, as in appearance
grimaced (v.): disagreeable look
grotto (n.): cave, tunnel
impediment (n.): delay, hindrance

impetuous (adj.): abrupt, impulsive, rash
impulse (adj.): notion, whim
indispensable (adj.): needful, required
inevitable (adj.): certain, sure to happen
interrogator (v.): examiner, questioner
intrigue (v.): curiosity, imagination
intuition (n.): insight, instinct
jeered (v.): mocked, ridiculed
keen (adj.): alert, sharp
labyrinth (n.): maze, network
libel (n.): unjust accusation
lingering (n.): slow and painful
meager (adj.): inadequate, slight
meted (v.): administered, measured out
mused (v.): considered, pondered
pensive (adj.): thoughtful, serious
peril (n.): hazard, risk
persuade (v.): convince, get
plummet (v.): rapid descent, fall
precocious (adj.): clever, quick
predicament (n.): difficult situation
providence (n.): foresight, provision
punctuated (v.): broken, interrupted
relayed (v.): communicated, passed along
rendezvous (n.): meeting, encounter
ruse (n.): blind, device
sage (n.): knowing, wise
scrutinized (v.): examined, investigated

shroud (n.): cover, screen, veil
specter (n.): ghostly form
spurious (adj.): fake, forged
starboard (adj.): right side of ship
stupefying (v.): dizzying, stunning
stupor (n.): apathy, daze
stymied (v.): hindered, frustrated
succumbed (v.): surrendered, yielded
sufficient (adj.): ample, adequate
surly (adj.): gruff, ill-natured
tarnation (adj.): damnation
terse (adj.): crisp, pointed
travesty (n.): shameful example
tributary (n.): branch of river
vague (adj.): dim, hazy, unclear
volatile (adj.): apt to erupt, unstable
zeal (n.): desire, eagerness

listen|imagine|view|experience

AUDIO BOOK DOWNLOAD INCLUDED WITH THIS BOOK!

In your hands you hold a complete digital entertainment package. Besides purchasing the paper version of this book, this book includes a free download of the audio version of this book. Simply use the code listed below when visiting our website. Once downloaded to your computer, you can listen to the book through your computer's speakers, burn it to an audio CD or save the file to your portable music device (such as Apple's popular iPod) and listen on the go!

How to get your free audio book digital download:

1. Visit www.tatepublishing.com and click on the e|LIVE logo on the home page.
2. Enter the following coupon code:
   63de-1f52-6075-455a-e1cf-b087-bf96-77e5
3. Download the audio book from your e|LIVE digital locker and begin enjoying your new digital entertainment package today!